TIME VILLAINS

MONSTER PROBLEMS

VICTOR PIÑEIRO

sourcebooks
young readers

Published by Sourcebooks Young Readers, an imprint of Sourcebooks
P.O. Box 4410, Naperville, Illinois 60567–4410
(630) 961-3900
sourcebooks.com

Cataloging-in-Publication Data is on file with the Library of Congress.

This product conforms to all applicable CPSC and CPSIA standards.

Source of Production: Versa Press, East Peoria, Illinois, United States
Date of Production: May 2022
Run Number: 5025862

Printed and bound in the United States of America.
VP 10 9 8 7 6 5 4 3 2 1

To Julian and Luke

1

I woke up Sunday night at 3:17 a.m. with a flying monkey slapping my face.

It hadn't been a great night. My sister, Brady, needed a sparring partner for her Brazilian jujitsu class, then my best friend Wiki needed someone to quiz him on quantum physics for fun. My body was mashed and my brain was mush. All I'd wanted that night was a twenty-course omakase sushi dinner and eight glorious hours of sleep. Instead I got burnt meat loaf and insomnia.

And an extremely unwelcome visitor. He must've been extra quiet, because I hadn't heard the window open or the creepy sound of wings flapping next to me. I was in the middle of pastrami dreams when I opened an eye and saw a silhouette standing on my chest. An enormous, hairy monkey silhouette. With epic wings. Slapping me with one hand and covering my mouth with the other.

"MMMMFFFFHHHMMNNN!" I screamed through his hand, which I hope he correctly translated to, "Couldn't you have knocked on the front door like a regular monkey? What's wrong with you? Are you too good for front doors?" He must have understood some of it, because he gave me the biggest monkey grin and then motioned to the door.

I followed him downstairs hoping and praying that he didn't wake up my parents. ("Oh hey Mom, meet my pal Billy. Hairy with wings? Nah, he just hit puberty early.") He led me to the front door and motioned for me to open it. Given the insanity of the situation, I was half expecting a beatboxing gorilla.

Principal Gale? She was drenched and had a desperate look in her eyes.

"Javi. Sorry for the rude awakening. I need a favor. Can I come in?"

Five minutes later, after she had a cup of tea and

apologized for the slappity-slap wake-up call, she laid it on me.

"Javi, I need to go home right now."

Maybe it was because it was the middle of the night, but I shook my head, confused. "Um, did you forget where you live? I guess I can draw you a map. It's not super far from here. Were you sleepwalking?"

She shook her head. "No, Javi. Not my house. My home."

Then it hit me. Oz. She wanted me to send her back to Oz. And yeah, believe it or not, my principal is Dorothy Gale and that was actually something I could do.

We made our way to the basement door, down the creaky stairs and to the cage. Under the stairway, hidden behind some old newspapers, was what looked like a super-fancy bird cage. The bars were thick and there wasn't a visible keyhole because—surprise!—it's literally impossible to open without the magic word. The last time we tried to open it, we were attacked by the same giant monkey that had just woken me up, plus fourteen of his pals. Good thing we were friends now.

"Here you go, Principal Gale," I whispered as I handed it to her. She opened her mouth to say the magic word, then looked at me for a second. The bell was in there— the one that lets us summon anyone from history or fiction like it's no big deal. She'd wrapped it tightly in cloth so that it was impossible to ring and had me change the cage's password every month. (After we kinda sorta summoned Blackbeard a few months ago, she wanted to make sure the bell didn't fall into the wrong hands.) She took one last serious look into my eyes and I smiled nervously. She hated my passwords.

"Chewy Chili Cheeseburger."

"Can you please stop letting Javi pick the password, Principal Gale?" My sister was coming down the stairs. "They get worse every month."

"Brady!" I yelled. "You do realize it's three in the morning, right?"

"You do realize that there's a flying monkey in my room playing with my dolls, right?"

"Touché. Good morning, Brady."

"I'm sorry about that," Gale said as she pulled the bell out of the cage and unwrapped it. "If this wasn't a complete emergency, I wouldn't be here at this time of night."

Brady nodded. "Do you miss the Cowardly Lion or something?"

She smiled a teensy bit before her face got serious again. "No, there's trouble at home, and I need you to send me back. Let's go."

We dashed up the stairs and into our dining room and there was Andy, purring loudly. Andy's not our cat, he's our table. It's a long story.

"Andy, it's been too long. I hope you're well. I really need to go home again. Not Kansas. My other home." Gale sat down at the head of the table and handed me the bell.

"I imagine it will take me exactly a month to take care of business at home," she said to Brady and me. "I need you to summon me again exactly one month from today. October 13. But not a day before. And Javi, Brady—allow absolutely no one to use Andy while I'm away. Promise me that."

We nodded and lifted up the bell, ready to ring it.

"Wait!" Brady said. "What about school?"

"I made last-minute preparations with key members of the faculty. They'll make sure the school is running smoothly while I'm away."

I raised my hand. "Who's going to be the new principal while you're gone?"

Gale smiled. "I left you in good hands."

I rang the bell, there was a loud poof, and Principal Gale disappeared. Everything got quiet for a second. Then Brady and I heard a noise and slowly turned to the kitchen. The flying monkey was sitting in our refrigerator scarfing down the meat loaf.

"Diespertate niñitos!" I shot awake to blaring music downstairs. It was almost as bad as the monkey slaps. "Time for school!" Mami was making all sorts of noise in the kitchen. I rolled out of bed with a thousand bags under each eye and moped my way down to the dining room, tossing myself into a chair and promptly falling half-asleep again. Then Mami jumped out from the kitchen and started slapping the table with her palms to the rhythm of the way-too-loud salsa music like it was a conga drum.

"Levantate, Javi! It's a sunny day outside. Dame una sonrisa!"

Meet Mami. She's like a five-foot-three battery that's

always charged to the point of exploding. You know that old nursery rhyme, "Girls are full of sugar and spice and everything nice"? Mami's full of professional-grade fireworks, marching-band cymbals, and heavy-metal drum solos. I swear, her blood is caffeine.

"Dónde está Brady? Brady! Up up up! Vamossssss!" She danced her way up the stairs, belting out whatever song was on, and knocked on her door to the beat of the music. It's like the whole house was her drum. Brady's even less of a morning person than I am, and I could hear her grunty moan from where I was sitting. "If I don't keep the rhythm going, you don't get to school on time. Come on! Let's go!"

Two minutes later Brady plunked down a bowl, dumped cereal into it and munched aggressively with the most gravelly look imaginable. The cereal slowly woke her up, and her devil glare softened into a mean-ish stare, which meant I could ask her questions without being turned to stone.

"When did Señor Hairywings finally leave?"

"Sunrise," she groaned. "After we perfected our dance routine. He's a talented monkey."

I whistled long and low. "Yikes. So who do you think the new principal's going to be?"

She munched in silence for a few seconds. "Ms. Kahlo? Ms. Sherry-Zadi? I can't think of another teacher who isn't out to lunch."

"I've got my fingers crossed for Ahab. Good old Mr. Scrimshaw would have us all wearing sailor outfits and wrestling whales in days." We laughed so hard that she spit out cereal.

"Whoa! Caramba. Which one of you destroyed the fridge?" Mami had the fridge door open and was looking inside like she was staring at a crime scene.

"That's our cue," I whispered, and Brady and I grabbed our backpacks and fled. As I shut the door I yelled, "A flying monkey hung out with us last night, and he got pretty hungry. He doesn't have great manners!" I've learned that the best way to handle questions like that are with the truth, because no one will ever believe it.

"The flying monkeys showed up last night?" Wiki said as he walked across our lawn. Wiki's my best friend and basically a brain with feet. If scientists ever tried to measure his smarts by attaching his head to a computer, the computer would explode.

"It's a long story," Brady said. "Let's get some distance from our house first, though. Before Mami finds out what the monkey did to the garage."

Brady, Wiki and I fast-walked up the trail next to our house until we saw the ginormous castle that happened to be our school.

"So then she says, 'I'm leaving you in good hands,' and—poof!—she's gone. Bye-bye principal." Brady was telling the whole story excitedly. I added in the part about the monkey slaps.

"This is troubling. Deeply troubling." Wiki rubbed his chin. Pretty much everything that didn't involve winning a lottery or petting puppies was deeply troubling to Wiki. The guy loved being deeply troubled. "There are no great candidates for principal that I can think of. No other natural leaders like Gale. No one to save us if something goes wrong. Oh." He stopped in his tracks. "Did she say anything about using Andy?"

Brady shrugged. "He's off limits to everyone else. She

made us swear it. Oh, do you know what Javi's password was this month?"

"I try not to—"

"Chewy chili cheeseburger!" I said, hoping for the teensiest smile.

Wiki rolled his eyes. Then we walked in silence for a little bit, and I wondered if Wiki was thinking about Gale, Andy, or the best cheese for a chili cheeseburger. (Alpine Lace Swiss, for the record.)

"A school without a leader. Without a protector. And that table sitting in your dining room, ready to ruin our lives again. Just when I thought the school year might be off to a good start." Wiki was in pure fret mode now. You could see the weight of the world push down onto his shoulders.

"Hey, one thing at a time," I said, trying to defuse his stress like I always did. "Let's just see who she picked as principal. Maybe we're all forgetting one amazing teacher. Maybe we'll love the new principal so much we'll want them to stay in charge." Wiki didn't seem convinced.

We split ways in the lobby, Wiki heading to the

bathroom while Brady followed me to my locker to grab the fancy calculator we shared. (Not like she needs it, but she likes the oohs and ahhs it gets from her friends, and there's no way Mami's buying us two of them.)

As we walked by the gym we passed all the trophy cases with little gold people kicking soccer balls and hitting baseballs on tiny pedestals. Why oh why did I take this route to my locker? This was always a guaranteed day-ruiner, and today was a day that had to be good.

I stopped right before we passed the last shelf, which had the one trophy that had nothing to do with sports or gym. On a big blue-and-white pillar stood a gold-wrapped sandwich in all its delectable glory. Finistere Sandwich-Making Champion: Reggie Donaldson. It stung every time I read that stupid name on that stupid trophy.

"An open-faced sandwich," I growled. "The nerve. I ask you, how can you win a sandwich-making contest with an open-faced sandwich? That's not even a sandwich! The entire point of a sandwich is that it's fillings sandwiched between something else. Plus, you're supposed to be able to eat it without a fork and knife. Reggie literally had little forks next to his open-faced sandwich for judges to try. How is that even a sandwich? That's like winning a pizza contest with a calzone!"

Losing sucks. Losing a contest you were sure you'd win sucks even more. But losing a contest that the faculty created for you as thanks for saving their school? That's the worst kind of suck. Yeah, after I'd saved Finistere from pirates with Brady and Wiki, the teachers granted us each one favor. Mine was that we have an annual sandwich-making competition, since there was a clear lack of food-related contests at our school, and my goal in life is being the universe's premier chef. Well, they obliged and did a pretty great job of making the contest a big deal. But when it finally happened, and I unveiled my Michelin-starred-restaurant-worthy pork belly tripleta sandwich (an extravagant twist on a Puerto Rican classic), the judges put it in third place. Third. Place. Only Ms. Vlad gave it a perfect score, and I'm pretty sure vampires can't eat, so she was faking it.

So now I'm not only a C+ student and a C+ athlete, I'm also a C+ chef. Which means I'm C+ at life. Javi Santiago:

the C+ human. I can't decide if that makes me incredibly angry or overwhelmingly sad. It probably means I'll end up jobless and friendless and living in my parents' basement until my existence is just a legend they tell kids on my block to freak them out. The Legend of Javi the Loser. Beware the talentless basement dweller.

"You know what else is an open-faced sandwich? Pizza. Do you think anyone in their right mind would let a pizza win a sandwich contest? What kind of world are we living in?" I threw my hands up in the air and let out an epic groan.

Brady was pretty patient when I went on my open-faced-sandwich rants. She patted me on the shoulder and gently nudged me back toward class.

The first half of the day went by like no one even realized Gale was gone. Partway through math class Wiki whispered, "Clearly you dreamt what happened last night. Did you and Brady just have the same dream?" Yeah, like people dream about flying monkeys destroying fridges all the time. Still, I was starting to worry that maybe the principal hadn't told anyone but us. Were they mounting a full-on search party for her? Were the cops involved? Gale seemed way too responsible to just ghost the entire school.

And then, at the end of math class, the intercom crackled and a very familiar voice came on. "Is this blasted thing on? Oops, tis indeed! Ahem, excuse me. Could everyone please assemble in the auditorium? All of you lads and lasses, make your way to the high school auditorium." My eyes went wide. Please tell me I was right, and Captain Ahab, our insane whale-hunter-turned-teacher, was about to become our new principal.

Everyone filed out of their classes confused and whispering to each other about what might have gone wrong. "Do you think a monster wrecked another class-room?" "Maybe more of those weird pirate-looking guys came snooping around our school?" "Hey, maybe Billy wasn't lying about that dragon he saw flying around here last year. Maybe he's back."

After the events of last year, involving loads of pirates, a dragon, a monster, and a full-scale pirate ship, Principal Gale made Brady, Wiki, and I swear to secrecy, but that didn't stop the rumors. No one knew the real secret of our school, though: that teachers here came from history or from stories, thanks to our magic table. It had been tough at first—we had almost died a few times, and you kinda have to talk out near-death experiences so you can process them—but the few times that we did slip up, no one believed us anyway, so it was fine. Still, going to school feels way different once you realize that your teachers might be four hundred years old, or only exist in books. But by the time this school year rolled around, we started taking it for granted.

"All right, you scurvy dogs, everyone in your seats, please!" Ahab was holding a megaphone, and I could practically imagine him screaming at his ship's crew the same way. "We have an important announcement and don't want to waste another moment!" Wiki and I sat next to each other, and Wiki put his head in his hands, too heavy to hold up with all the worries in it. Brady sat with her fourth grade class a few rows down and turned to give us a knowing look.

"Perhaps some of you have noticed a certain someone missing today? No, Principal Gale isn't sick. She's not suffering from consumption or the grippe." (I think that means having a cold.) "Our dear principal had to leave suddenly to take care of a family emergency far away."

The auditorium gasped all at once, probably because none of us could remember a single day that Gale wasn't at school. She had perfect attendance, and since no one remembered when she started, it was probably perfect attendance for three hundred years. Everyone started chattering about it until Ahab loudly cleared his throat.

"Now, she should be back soon enough. Probably in the next few weeks. But in the meantime, we're going to have a substitute principal lead the school. Principal Gale chose the replacement herself. She's truly...um, great...and definitely an interesting choice..."

Uh-oh. Ahab wasn't too psyched about Gale's pick. Wiki, Brady, and I all braced ourselves for what was coming next. I quickly ran through the worst options for principal in my head. Dr. Jekyll would be pretty boring. Don Quixote was way too weird to lead anything. Ms. Sherry-Zadi would spend way too much time telling never-ending stories. Oh. Oh wait. There was one nightmare pick. But there was no way Principal Gale would choose—

"Ms. Vlad, ladies and gentlemen. Ms. Vlad is your new principal."

No. Way.

Ms. Vlad? Ms. Vlad is a vampire. I mean, literally a vampire. She drinks blood out of a thermos. She hates sunlight. She once turned into a giant vampire bat. Oh, and she's the strictest, meanest teacher at Finistere, by far. Ms. Vlad as a principal was your worst nightmare's worst nightmare. This was bad. This was really, really bad.

And I wasn't the only one who thought so. The entire auditorium went silent. Completely hear-a-pin-drop silent. Looking around the room, everyone's jaw was practically on the floor. Ahab could have transformed into a giant squid and we wouldn't have been more shocked. Then I very clearly heard one little girl start crying.

Ms. Vlad clomped up to the stage, her face looking like it had never tried a smile in its whole life. She pushed away Ahab's megaphone, knowing that everyone would listen to her even if she whispered. After a dramatic pause, she spoke.

"There will be a few changes here, under my watch.

I will announce them soon. Now please exit the auditorium in perfect silence."

It was like we were in a silent movie. You couldn't even hear people's footsteps as we left the auditorium. For a minute, the world felt like all the color had been sucked out of it. Everyone looked at each other like they were suddenly exhausted.

"Welcome to the new Finistere," Wiki mumbled to me. "Brace yourself."

The change was almost immediate. Finistere
felt like a zombie wasteland crossed with an extra-sad
funeral. Everyone either looked like they were on the
verge of tears or scared for their lives.

The first thing Vlad changed, which affected everything else, was the way detention worked. Principal Gale
didn't believe in detention. Usually she just brought
the bad kid to her office and they talked out what the
offender had done wrong. Her tough-but-fair attitude
straightened them up quick. But Ms. Vlad hated talking
to people, and she had exactly zero patience for anyone
breaking even the tiniest rule. So she made some big
changes.

Anyone who did anything wrong—I'm not talking about starting a fight or pantsing someone, I mean even talking above a whisper in the hallways or chewing too loudly at lunch—had to serve detention with the high school gym teacher, Mr. Cimmerian. And he was legendary. Take the strongest guy you've ever seen and multiply that by three or four. His muscles practically ripped his clothes. And he never cracked a smile. In fact, whenever he looked at you, you got the sense that he was figuring out the most efficient way to kill you. Back when we realized that our teachers weren't exactly local, Wiki figured out a few of their secret identities. Mr. Cimmerian was almost definitely Conan the Barbarian. Yeah, the dude who wields the giant ax and looks like he could rip you in half using just his pinkies. That was our detention monitor.

So the entire school was basically like Ms. Vlad's classroom: completely silent and drab and lifeless, chock-full of fear, and completely out of hope or joy. Sometimes I thought I was going deaf, but there was just nothing to hear except very quiet footsteps.

"T-H-I-S N-E-E-D-S T-O S-T-O-P" Wiki signed to

me. A few years ago we'd learned the alphabet in sign language so we could talk in class, but over the last week we'd gotten really good at it. We were sitting next to each other in the cafeteria, so signing back and forth felt ridiculous, but it was either that or Conan.

"A-M-E-N. B-U-T H-O-W?"

He shrugged and shook his head. Yeah, there was no obvious plan to make things better. Gale had told us we couldn't summon her back yet, and none of the other teachers seemed to want to challenge Vlad's dictatorship. But now that it had been a week, and the awfulness had really sunk in, I was ready to talk about it with the teachers I trusted.

Like every year at Finistere, I had an interesting crop of teachers. Some were nice, a couple were great, there were a few duds, but all were supremely weird. But of seventh grade's lineup, my clear favorite was Mr. Lofting, my science teacher. Seventh grade was life science: animals, plants, pretty much anything that wasn't rocks or lava or space. And Mr. Lofting's class was like a zoo. Ever since we were in elementary school Wiki and I had been curious about it, because you could hear the animals as you passed his classroom. Kids said he had tigers and elephants in there, and that a kid once got eaten by a crocodile. Walking in on the first day of school I was a tad worried, but there were no human-eating animals in there. Just awesome ones.

The star of Mr. Lofting's class was Polynesia, his big blue-and-yellow macaw. She was loud and knew way more English than a parrot should and actually seemed to understand what we were saying in class every once in a while. She also had a pretty great sense of humor for an animal. Then there was Chee-Chee the monkey. We were afraid of him at first—I mean, who's ever seen a chimpanzee outside a zoo? But he turned out to be super chill, the opposite of those circus monkeys who jump all around and steal your peanuts. He would just kind of walk around the classroom and check in on everyone with a pat on the back and a nod, like he was your life coach. My personal favorite was Dab-Dab, Mr. Lofting's pet duck. What is it about ducks that make them so over-the-top hilarious? Dab-Dab was next level, though—he would hop on your desk and stare you down. And when somebody said something wrong or stupid Dab-Dab would sometimes quack, like he was saying, "Hey, shut up." I would have adopted that duck in a second.

But what was somehow even wilder than the animals wandering his classroom were the ones perched outside it. Lofting's class was on the second floor, and flocks of birds were always gathered right outside it, constantly chattering among themselves. Sometimes a family of squirrels would hang out on the window ledge for an entire class too. The dude was an animal magnet like I've never seen. I wanted to know his secret.

"Okay class, ten more minutes before the bell rings. Let's get those food-web dioramas to a good place. We only have one more class period to devote to them," Mr. Lofting said as he helped Sally glue her apex predator to her shoebox. He had a prim English accent that made him even more endearing. Wiki and I were arguing over whether we should put one of my action figures at the top of our desert food web, and I was getting annoyed.

"Dude, don't people always say that humans are at the top of the food chain? You don't see anyone eating humans. We belong at the top."

"Javi, how often have you eaten a desert fox or eagle?

How do you propose this works—humans driving through this desert hunt down foxes and eagles and cook them for dinner?"

"Look, I just think it's weird not to have humans in a food web. I'm putting this guy right here." I started sticking tape on the action figure's boots to put him at the far corner of our shoebox diorama when the action figure was grabbed from my hand and thrown to the floor—by Dab-Dab. The duck gave me a look like he was scolding me. Quack quack.

"Dab-Dab, I'm the apex predator in this situation. Aren't you supposed to be afraid of me?" He quacked at me a few more times, pointing at the shoebox and shaking his little duck head. "I'm pretty sure I'm right, duck." That just made him quack louder and angrier. "Oh, I can't stay mad at you, Dab-Dab." I pet him a little and he gave me a "Don't patronize me" look before he hopped off the table. Wiki gave me the most self-satisfied smile.

A few minutes later everyone exited the class, and I hung around until it was empty. Mr. Lofting looked up to see me at his desk. "Ah, Javi. How are you, sir? Anything

I can help you with?" Usually asking a teacher if they hated the principal was an awkward question, but since Mr. L was so warm and nice, I cut right to the chase.

"Mr. Lofting, are you and the other teachers okay with the new, um…direction the school has taken since Principal Gale left?"

He chuckled. "A bit lifeless lately, eh? More of a prison than a place of learning."

"Yes!" I said. "You get it. Of course you do. So, how are you guys okay with it?"

He shrugged. "If she was to be our forever principal, I would definitely consider other employment opportunities. But this is only for a number of weeks. The blink of an eye, really. The teachers mostly find it amusing, and it'll make for a great story years from now. Just blink and it'll be over, Mr. Santiago. Just blink."

I walked to art class in a funk. I sometimes forget that adults and kids experience time totally differently. A month to an adult seems to last an hour. Maybe two. And years seem to fly by for them too. Mami and Papi sometimes say things like, "Can you believe it's January again?" Of course I believe it! A bajillion things happened in the last twelve months, and life is 100 percent different than it was last January, which feels like a century ago! Heck, it's only been four months since I was facing down a dragon and a monster in our high school's basement. Life moves *slow*.

So the teachers weren't going to be any help. They would just hibernate in their classrooms for the next month and collect stories to tell Principal Gale for a laugh. You know how time goes by when you're having fun? Well, the opposite is even more true. A month in the abyss lasts a hundred lifetimes. I wasn't about to put up with a hundred lifetimes of Principal Vamp's regime. We had to do something, and the sooner the better.

"¿Javi, que pasa? Your heart looks like it's crying." Ms. Calderon patted my back as I walked into art class. Ms. Calderon was secretly none other than Frida Kahlo, one of the most famous artists of all time. "¿Es la principal, no?"

I nodded my head. Yep. It's the principal. "I can't take this much longer, Ms. C. This is like medieval torture."

She smiled knowingly. "Ms. Vlad has a very different leadership style than Principal Gale, but they both have their pros and cons. I don't love it either, of course," she said with a wink, "but it's only for—"

"—a month, I know, I know. People keep telling me that." I took my place behind my easel next to Wiki. We were working on a farm landscape, and I was almost done with it, so I started painting a squid-headed giant monster wrecking the barns and eating the livestock. It was pretty therapeutic.

Wiki looked over at it and gave me a slow nod. "You're ready to do something about it. I can tell. Whenever you start inserting squid monsters into your art, it means it's time to act."

"Dying to do something about it. But I can't figure out what we can do. The teachers don't seem to care, so they'll be no help. We can't bring Gale back early. I doubt we're going to sweet-talk Vlad into easing up. I'm at a loss."

Wiki painted his boring landscape for a few minutes. His computer brain was processing. Finally he turned to me again. "We're what's called information-poor. We need more information before we can construct a plan. We need to find out more about Ms. Vlad and what makes her tick."

"Hmm, yeah, that makes sense. So do you want us to talk to Ms. Vlad's friends? Because obviously she doesn't have any. I doubt she even talks to anyone unless she's commanding them to do something. So if we want to read her mind, we're going to have to find someone with a shrink ray that can make us small enough so we can crawl through her ear and get to her brain. Wow, this is going to be complicated..."

"Javi, I'm talking about gathering intel. She's a closed book, but maybe we'll figure something out if we talk to other teachers. Find out what makes her tick. Work out why—"

"Javier Santiago, please report to the principal's office immediately," the intercom blared.

"What?" I squeaked. Did Vlad hear us talking about her? Was the room bugged? I gulped hard and nodded somberly to Wiki. "Welp, see you in the afterlife, amigo."

I shuffled out of the room in a daze, walking down three hallways before I realized I was walking toward the bathroom. Like I said. C+ brain. C+ human. We were doomed.

4

I walked down the middle school halls whistling a funeral dirge, wondering if I could stop by the janitor's closet and grab a shovel to dig my own grave. Why would Ms. Vlad want to see me, of all people? I knew Mr. Lofting and Ms. Kahlo wouldn't have ratted me out. Was it Dab-Dab? Maybe Vlad was in cahoots with the duck. I knew I should've shared my lunch with him last week. Always be nice to waterfowl—that was my new life lesson.

"Javi, might you be lost?" I turned to see Ms. Love walking a few feet behind me. Ms. L was the other highlight of seventh grade. She taught coding, which I figured would mean sitting in front of computers until our eyes bled, but her class had more of a robo-hacking, mad scientist vibe. Her proper British accent contrasted nicely with her savage bookworm vibe. "That was your name on the intercom, yes? If you're looking for the principal's office, I'm afraid it moved."

Of course Vlad didn't take Principal Gale's office. It was way too bright and magical. I should've known. "Where is it exactly?" I asked.

A normal teacher would give directions, or tell you what classroom it was next to. But the best teachers at Finistere are the least normal ones. She smiled at me and snapped four times. A low whirring sound became louder, and then zooming around the corner, one of her signature tiny drones appeared. It flew to Ms. L and hovered by her head. "Can you please take Javi to Vlad's new office?" she asked. It bobbed in the air like it was nodding. "Follow that drone, Javi. And good luck." I nodded and she disappeared into a classroom. The drone zoomed down the hallway.

"Wait for me!" I called after it, sprinting to catch up. "Okay, slow down the pace. Running gets us detention these days." It did another bob-nod and led me down a few halls at a less speedy pace. Then we made the transition between the middle and high school, opening a normal door to walk into an ancient stone passageway.

Mami once asked, "Do you ever get used to seeing that thing from our backyard?" And no, no one ever did. Sure, plenty of people can see their school from their backyard, but most people's school isn't an enormous medieval castle time-warped into a suburban neighborhood. Finistere's high school has stone walls, spires, a repurposed dungeon, and probably used to house a bunch of knights and a beardy old king who said things like, "Extra crumpets for Sir Galahad!" Or, "Off with his head!" Our middle school is more boring than you can imagine, and our high school is more awesome. I have no idea how high schoolers can concentrate on anything except the epic sword fights that probably went down in their classrooms.

"Um, where are you taking me, Twirly?" The little hoverbot was leading me down a long spiral stairway until we hit the bottom. Finistere's basement. The last time I was down here Blackbeard summoned a massive pirate ship. But that was in the pool, in another area. I'd never been in this part of the school, and this had to be where the dungeon used to exist. Other than a couple of barely lit torches, it was pitch black, dank as dank could be, and, maybe I was wrong, but I think it faintly smelled like death. Either that or really old cheese. In any event, I almost puked. Keep it together, Javi. You're just walking through a pitch-black dungeon on your way to get murdered by a vampire. NBD.

The drone flew all the way down the hall, then took a right. It got darker with every step, and when I finally hung a right I was basically walking into complete darkness. There was a tiny glow in the distance, but I thought I might be making it up. Keep walking, Javi. Step. Step. Step. Just keeping walking until you inevitably fall into the huge hole you can't see. Thankfully there was no dramatic drop to my death. Instead everything got really quiet and I practically tiptoed down the hall—no idea why. When I was almost there, the perfect silence was settled all around me and—"Beeeeep!" I practically screamed as the hoverbot sped forward.

"Twirly! Shh! Patience. I'm not exactly skipping through a park on a sunny day."

There's a saying in Spanish: "Era tan oscuro como la boca de un lobo." It was as dark as the inside of a wolf's mouth. Yep, that's exactly how dark and terrifying it was. I felt like I was walking down its tongue and past rows of his enormous fangs as he closed his mouth. And then the glowing thing was right in front of me and I realized it was a tiny bit of light coming from behind a door. A door that I almost slammed into. Okay, here I am. This is it, Javi. Open the door and have a look around. "Beep beep!" The drone hovered in front of my face for a second, then flew back into the darkness. Way to abandon me in my time of need, Twirly.

I inhaled all the courage I could and pushed open the door. Oh. Wow. Yeah, Ms. Vlad's office was the exact opposite of Principal Gale's. Gale's office was awesome and vaguely magical but still warm and put you in a good mood. Vlad's was something between a mausoleum, a cemetery, and the inside of a troll's belly button. If I could describe it in a word, it would be *Death*. If I could describe it in six words they would be *Death death death death death death*. The walls were bare and cave-like, her "desk" was a big stone that looked like a place human sacrifices went down, and in the back there was what any other student would think was a big wooden box, but I knew was nothing less than a coffin. Why did Gale pick this murderous psychopath to be our principal?

Calm down, Javi. "Um, Ms. Vlad?" I croaked. She was nowhere to be seen. I walked around the office a few times, but except for two rickety-looking wooden chairs, it was almost completely empty. The only thing I noticed was what looked like black paint on her desk. Wait, was that dried blood? I got a full-body shiver. Then as I peeked into her empty coffin, I realized that Vlad didn't just work here, she probably lived here too. That gave me an even bigger shiver, tippy-top of the head all the way down to my little toe. I walked back to the door, then turned around to give the room a final look.

"Javi. Looking for me?" Ms. Vlad's voice came from a few inches behind me, and I screamed so loud I was surprised the castle didn't crumble. I flipped around, and my shriek was frozen on my face. Ms. Vlad's stern expression didn't even shift. I guess she was used to people screaming in her face. Comes with being a murderous vampire.

"Please, have a seat." She sat down behind her sacrificial "desk" and stared me down. Has a principal ever murdered a student? I guess there was a first time for everything. "There is something I wanted to discuss with you." She paused and gave me another look. "Is everything okay?"

Okay? Our school turned into Nightmare Land, and I'm hanging out in a dungeon with a vampire two feet from a sacrificial table! Chill, Javi, you're a master at playing things off. Is everything okay? Give the perfect answer in 3-2-1...

"Why do they call them 'bats' in English? In Spanish they're murcielago. It's such an awesome word. In English you could be talking about a wooden stick. 'Bat.' It's weird. A baseball bat is nothing like a flying bat. But in Spanish, mur-ciel-a-go. I love the way it sounds. I love bats, by the way. Big fan of bats. They're majestic."

Bravo, Javi. Yet another home run in a life of home runs. Ms. Vlad eyed me like she was honestly concerned I might be insane.

"Well, I have a question for you. But perhaps it would be better if your friends were here too." She took a walkie-talkie off her belt, which almost looked funny in this medieval sacrifice room, and spat, "Will Green, Brady Santiago to the principal's office at once." I wonder if she realized that literally no one knew where the new principal's office was. "Let us wait until they arrive."

Then came the awkwardest five minutes of my life. Vlad pulled her thermos out of her bag and placed it on her lap. Then, without taking her eyes off me for a milli-second, spent the next five minutes silently staring at me with her usual death stare as she took sips from her thermos. And to be clear, her thermos was full of blood. Blood! And she knew I knew that. Yep, my principal was drinking blood and staring me down in a converted murder room next to her coffin bed. Totally normal school stuff.

"So, this weather lately. Wild, right? Clouds...or, sun, maybe? I can't remember. Anyway, I've been super into pretzels recently. Not just the ones you buy in jars, but pretzel rolls, giant pretzels, all kinds. Sometimes I even take string cheese and I twist it in a pretzel-like fashion. You'd think that making it look more pretzel-like wouldn't change its flavor, but you'd be surprised." Twelve years old, still garbage at small talk. She didn't even pretend to listen or try to respond. Just sip, sip, sip that blood, and stare, stare, stare me down. Did time stop all of a sudden? Did God just hit pause on the whole universe?

"Hello?" Wiki peeked his head into the chamber. Bless you, Wiki! My savior. He walked in slowly and stood next to my chair. Brady was with him too. Vlad stared at us a few more seconds without any response, then put down her thermos.

5

"Thank you for coming on such short notice."
She looked at Wiki's expression. "This is not a disci-
plinary meeting. I have a question to ask you. A...favor."

A real-life vampiress wants us to do her a favor.
Chance that this is going to go well: negative infinity
percent. Chance that this is going to be horrible and lead
to our extremely painful demise: three billion percent.
(I was never great at percents, to be fair.)

"You are aware that most schools have vice principals, correct?" We nodded at the same time. I'd never
really thought about the fact that Finistere didn't. I
guess Gale's just that great a principal. No surprise.

"Good. I need help during my short tenure as principal. I am seeking a vice principal. Someone to help me run the school in Principal Gale's absence." We nodded more. Makes sense. I bet vampires don't go to principal school that often; she could use the help. "The problem is, there are no good candidates here."

Hmm. No good candidates? I could tell all three of us were running through options in our head. "Well, what about..." Brady said, and then took a long pause. "No. Not him. Definitely not her. No, that's a bad idea too. Okay, I see what you mean. Not a lot of teachers here are vice principal material." I chuckled at the thought of Ahab or Don Quixote as vice principal. And even though Frida Kahlo would be great, I knew she and Ms. Vlad weren't exactly besties.

"Why don't you put up a job posting on the internet?" Wiki asked. "I'm sure there are plenty of vice principals out there who would prefer working in a castle."

She shook her head quickly. "If they found out our school's secret, it would be catastrophic. No. Here is my proposition. I would like to invite a vice principal to our school from elsewhere." Um, isn't that what Wiki just recommended? Wiki's eyes were wide. Oh, elsewhere elsewhere. She wanted to use Andy.

"Absolutely not," Wiki said flatly. "Gale specifically made us promise not to summon anyone while she was away." Wow, Wiki, way to stand up to authority.

"Using the table to summon strangers for our amusement, yes. She would not approve of that. But this is for the betterment of the school. And she always wants to raise the quality of our school."

"Good point," Brady said. "Maybe there's a little wiggle room if it's for Finistere."

"No. There's zero wiggle room," Wiki huffed. "Did you guys already forget what happened four months ago? If Gale says no summoning, there's no summoning at all."

For Wiki, breaking the rules was like breaking your bones: avoid it at all costs. Vlad didn't look too happy.

"I understand your concern, Wiki, and I respect your wish to follow Gale's rule to the letter. But I am not asking you to summon another Blackbeard. I am asking you to invite an old friend of mine." I almost fell out of my chair—Ms. Vlad has friends? "A brilliant friend. Old and wise but strong and charismatic enough to help lead a school."

"Santa Claus?" I asked. She glared at me. I should stop thinking out loud.

"I'm sorry, Ms. Vlad—er, Principal Vlad. We can't help you," Wiki said. "When Gale returns, maybe you can invite this friend and make him vice principal."

Ms. Vlad got quiet, sat down, took a few sips of her blood thermos, and nodded like our transaction was complete. "Very well. I urge you to please consider my offer. Keep in mind that if I find someone I trust to help me, I can...loosen the reins here."

I liked the sound of that. "We'll talk it over," I said, nodding awkwardly the whole time as I backed out of her room slowly. Wiki and Brady followed me. We didn't say a word until we were out of the castle and back in the middle school.

"Did anyone else experience the past ten minutes, or did I go completely delusional?" Wiki asked, checking his forehead temperature.

"Guys, that was a coffin," Brady said, poking each of us in the chest for emphasis. "A coffin in her office. Even if she wanted us to summon Gandhi, I wouldn't trust someone who brings a coffin to a school."

"I'm pretty sure that's where she lives," I said. "And I'm also pretty sure her desk is some kind of sacrifice table. That black stuff on it looked like dried blood."

"Go against Principal Gale's one rule," Wiki moaned. "If anyone's a rule follower it's Vlad. She must be desperate to get help."

"Well, it doesn't matter if she's desperate," Brady said. "Obviously we're going to say no. Duh."

"Can you say no to your principal?" I asked. "Is that even legal? And if it is, how's she's going to treat us if we do?" I paused. "Poopy. She's going to treat us super-duper poopy."

We walked in silence, realizing exactly how bad our current situation was, and how many Conan detentions we were about to experience in a row. Finally Wiki piped up again.

"Oh no. I dropped one of my AirPods. Dad is going to kill me." He searched around on the floor. "I must have done it in Ms. Vlad's office."

"Wiki, did you just accidentally bug our principal's office?" Brady was clearly impressed.

Wow, every student's dream. "Wait," I said, grabbing Wiki's phone. "I hear something." Something that made no sense. Sobbing. "Listen to this." I turned up the volume and we all leaned in really close to hear it.

It was Ms. Vlad, and she was crying.

"My dear friend, I am so lonely without you. I thought this year would be better than the rest, but no longer. It is hopeless. We are never to be together. And the world won't know what a hero you actually are." She broke down into sobs.

We stood there listening to her cry for a long time, and when we finally snapped out of it, none of us could form a sentence for the rest of the walk home.

6

I was scrubbing school toilets with a crusty
old toothbrush when I reconsidered Vlad's offer. "You
know, our principal is feeling blue. Maybe the right
thing to do is help cheer her up. Be good Samaritans,
get some karma, practice random acts of kindness,
et cetera."

"Javi," Wiki said, as he mopped the nasty floors with
a tiny, raggedy mop, "why do I get the feeling that your
intentions are less than selfless?"

"Ugh!" Brady said as she cleaned something disgusting out of a sink, dropping her teeny bottlebrush and
crossing her arms. "I'm with Javi. Nothing is worth
cleaning duty every Tuesday."

Tidy-Up Tuesday. Vlad announced it the morning after our little chat, and we couldn't help but think it might be related. No more recess on Tuesdays; instead, kids would play janitor for that period and make every nook and cranny in Finistere spotless. Of course the three of us got bathroom duty. And of course all the good brushes and mops had already gone to other kids.

"Trust me. Inviting Vlad's acquaintances to our school would be far worse than any prison-like regimens she gives us," Wiki said. "Otherwise, she would have convinced Gale years ago and that person would already be here."

"Wiki, you're the dude who invited Blackbeard here in the first place," Brady huffed. "*Trust* isn't a word that should be coming out of your mouth." Wiki gritted his teeth and got back to mopping the gunk behind the toilets.

Hours later, I was home and getting out of the shower, hoping I'd cleaned off all the nastiness of Toilet Tuesday, when I heard Brady talking downstairs. "So that's the situation. Either we help our vampire principal or she keeps making our lives misery. I thought you might have some good advice."

What was she doing telling our parents about our bloodsucking principal? Had Brady cracked? I raced down the stairs and froze when I got to the dining room. Oh. This was much worse.

Sitting at the table was an Egyptian queen decked out in sparkling jewelry, a twelve-year-old version of the most famous musician of all time, and a strange-looking feline. Two of them were friends of ours. "Kid Mozart! Cleopatra! What a wonderful surprise!" I hugged them both, then waltzed over to Brady and whispered, "Hey. Guess what? This is literally the one thing you weren't supposed to do."

"Nope, wrong-o. Gale clearly told us not to let other people summon folks through Andy. She didn't say anything about us. Plus, these are our most trusted friends! Who better to give us advice?" I guess she kind of sort of had a point there?

"I have met this Vlad before, no?" Cleopatra asked. "The one who transformed into a giant bat?" Brady and I nodded. "She has a strong moral compass, that one. If she was making a request of me, I would comply. Perhaps you should consider her offer."

"I concur," Kid Mozart said. "She did not smile very much, but Mistress Vlad was decidedly on the side of good. Especially when we started tussling with those pirates."

The cat Brady had summoned hopped into Mozart's lap, purring and preening itself. "Hello, kitten! I am afraid I have not made your acquaintance."

"Oh no, Brady," I groaned. "Are you summoning the president's pets again?"

"I'm afraid not, dear boy," a voice said. Where was it coming from? "I'm more of a residential cat than a presidential cat. Though I reside nowhere, to be quite fair. Hee hee hee!" It was the cat. The cat who turned to me with a toothy smile bigger than my entire face. And then vanished into thin air.

We all screamed in unison. "Brady, who did you invite?" The cat's mouth materialized out of nowhere, right on top of my head, and then the rest of his body followed. We all screamed louder.

"Perhaps you'd like an introduction, but I'd rather you

make your own deduction. You know I'm feline, that's half the solution. Dear queen, perhaps you can make a contribution?"

Cleopatra smiled. "If only I could bring you to my palace. We revere all cats, for we know they are magic and royalty, but there are those outside our kingdom that disagree. You would prove your kind's superiority to the entire world."

The cat then dissolved into the air and appeared in Brady's arms. Brady gave him a big hug. "You chose your advisors with some precision. But you need no advice, you've made your decision. It's the greatest pleasure to meet this quartet, but I am afraid I have to jet. Toodles!"

The lunatic cat grinned his biggest grin yet, teleported to the couch, did a cartwheel, then vanished again. There was dead silence while we all whipped our heads from side to side waiting for him to reappear. After a solid three seconds, there was a tap at the back window. He was on the other side. He gave us a wink and a wave and vanished again.

"Brady, that better not be some demonic cat you just let loose into the world!" I yelled. "We're not having another Blackbeard situation—especially this early in the school year."

All eyes were on Brady, who laughed and shrugged. "He's even wackier than in the book! That's just the Cheshire Cat. From *Alice in Wonderland*. He's as harmless as it gets. Just kooky." The last *Alice in Wonderland* creature I'd met was a ginormous dragon who tried to burn me alive, so I wasn't super thrilled about it and she could tell. "Chill, Javi, I'm sure he'll show up later. I'll leave a bowl of milk out tonight."

"That unhinged smile just better not appear in my room after dark."

There was an awkward silence between the four of us. Then Kid Mozart walked over to the piano and sat down. "Perhaps this little ditty I composed for the princess of Vienna will help you mull over your dilemma. Feel free to add lyrics, if you'd like."

Cleopatra started singing along, belting out lyrics in an epic opera voice. I was glad our parents were visiting Abuela. After we got used to the high notes—which I was pretty sure would shatter all the glass in our house—Brady sat next to me.

"I think everyone but Wiki agrees. Tomorrow, let's get Vlad her vice principal."

I nodded. No more Toilet Tuesdays ever again.

7

The next morning I woke up to the sound of the bell ringing. It might as well have been an entire marching band squeezed into my room and playing their loudest. I shot awake in a cold sweat and practically jumped to the first floor.

"Javi! Brady! It's wake-up time!" Dad was ringing the bell like he was the town crier. One ring from that bell plus someone's name or picture on Andy equaled that person summoned to our dining room. Immediately my mind started playing mini movies of worst-case scenarios.

1. Brady left a picture of a dinosaur on the table and

there was a full-sized T. rex patiently waiting for us in the dining room.

2. Dad's newspaper was open to the sports page and an entire football team was crowded around Andy, hungry and cranky.

3. I left that list of crushes I scribbled the other night on Andy, and my top ten crushes were about to see me in my unicorn onesie pj's.

I grabbed the bell from Dad's hand a little too firmly but tried to play it off so he wouldn't ask questions. "So loud! Heh heh. Well, I'm up, and I heard Brady get up too."

No dinosaurs or cute girls in the dining room. Whew.

"Javi, how many times have I told you, if you open the windows late at night, you've got to close them. It's not August anymore—the entire first floor is freezing."

Hmm, that wasn't me—must've been Brady. I shivered through my breakfast and gave Brady the coldest glare when she sat down. When she gave me an innocent look,

I pointed to the bell. Our Cleopatra/Mozart karaoke fest had ended pretty abruptly when our parents came home, but this was next-level carelessness. She glared twice as hard and pointed back at me, mouthing, *This is your fault*. Oh. I vaguely remembered telling her I'd lock up the bell last night. I guess we could share the blame.

I had to come up with all sorts of dumb conversations on the way to school so that Wiki didn't ask about our evening or mention Ms. Vlad. I didn't feel like lying, and I definitely wasn't in the mood to argue again.

"So it turns out that the open-faced sandwich was invented because people used stale bread as plates in the olden days. Plates! They would always throw the bread away, but then some genius thought, hey! Why not eat the bread too? So eating an open-faced sandwich is like scarfing down a meal and then eating the soggy plate too. How disgusting is that? I'll tell you one thing. Those things are abominations and definitely not sandwiches."

"Javi, when will you stop with the open-faced sandwich rants?" Wiki groaned. "Can't you just face the fact that Reggie Donaldson bested you? Those little Scandinavian shrimp sandwiches were incredible.

Look, it doesn't mean that you won't win next year. Or that you're a bad cook. Just drop it. Move on."

"Never," I mumbled, feeling the rain cloud in my brain grow. "I'll never let this mockery of justice and good taste go. My name has been besmirched forevermore."

Wiki moaned, and I half wished I hadn't brought it up, but I'd successfully filled our entire commute with sando talk, so it was worth the sacrifice. Brady gave me a subtle thumbs-up as we walked into the school.

"Can all you lads and lasses make your way to the auditorium? We've got a special announcement first thing in the morning," Ahab announced on the loudspeaker. Wow, this was a weird time for a full school assembly. Brady and I raised our eyebrows at each other, and Wiki looked panicked as we made our way through the middle school and to the auditorium.

"Do you think Gale is back?" "Do you think Ms. Vlad is going to chain us to our desks now?" "Do you think Ms. Vlad is bringing the military to enforce her rules?" Everyone around us was trying to figure out why we were having another big announcement. Wiki was asking questions too but his were even darker and scarier.

"Ladies and gentlemen, boys and girls, I hope you are all having a wonderful morning on this beautiful day."

All the noise got sucked out of the room. It was perfect silence. And everyone's eyes were saucers. That sentence was just uttered by none other than Ms. Icy-Heart Murder-Eyes Vlad. She was wearing a huge smile that looked so fake I was wondering if there were puppet strings above her pulling at her mouth. This was really good news, but this was also really, really unsettling.

"I want to introduce you to your new vice principal, the brilliant, kind, magnificent Mr. Dragon. I hope you'll be as thrilled to meet him as I was, and you'll appreciate the new rules he'll put in place for the school."

A suave guy in a crisp suit with slicked-back gray hair, a long gray mustache, and perfect posture glided onto the stage. He was even more dapper and handsome and regal as he bowed to the audience and waved to the students with a big smile on his face. Who was this dude? The students were still quiet, but I could hear a lot of whispering from the teachers.

"Where did she find this guy?" Wiki whispered. "And so quickly. Maybe she actually took my advice?"

Brady and I gave each other a look. We wouldn't have to go behind Wiki's back and summon Vlad's friend—crisis averted!

"It is a pleasure to meet you all. I have heard the most wonderful things about you," the man said in a low, soothing voice. "I look forward to guiding this school to greatness while I am here. As Ms. Vlad said, I am a big believer in happy students being great students, which means more recess, more desserts at lunch, and zero homework."

The guy might as well have said he was giving each of us a million bucks. Every student practically leapt out of their seat, clapping like they wanted to break every bone in their hands and roaring and cheering like they wanted to lose their voices. I doubt it'll ever get that loud in that auditorium again. It was madness. Mr. Dragon let all of the applause wash over him and just waited patiently until it died down, which took a long, long time.

"You will begin seeing these changes very soon. In the meantime, I hope to meet each and every one of you. I will be making the rounds today and introducing myself to each of you during lunch and recess. I look forward to a happy school that you're all excited to come to every day. Good day, my friends."

"Mr. D! Mr. D! Mr. D!" the school chanted as they left the auditorium rowdier than even Principal Gale would ever be okay with. Brady and I high-fived, but Wiki was lost in thought. We let the mob go in front of us and then started our way back to our homerooms, the halls echoing with joyous screams and epic hollering.

"You guys didn't summon Mr. Dragon...did you?" Wiki asked quietly.

"No way!" Brady said as I shook my head. "He's gotta be local."

"Whew. Okay, good." Wiki's brain fluttered off to other worries.

We were halfway down the stone hall that exited the high school when someone tapped me on the shoulder. It was Ms. Vlad, still wearing that impossible grin.

"I wanted to thank you three for your excellent advice. One of our faculty members had a trusted friend who was vice principal at a nearby school. He seems like a promising addition to Finistere, no?"

"You did good, Ms. Vlad. You did real good."

8

The next week was too good to be true. First, Mr. Dragon must have convinced Vlad to get rid of detention, so no more Conan staring kids down and traumatizing them for life. Then the new vice principal announced that it was important for kids to socialize between classes, so the hallways became fun again. And even though he said he was still working with teachers to get us more recess time, he did let it start whenever you were finished with lunch, so instead of sitting at tables awkwardly waiting for the bell to ring, we'd just inhale our lunches in two seconds and then have double recess. There were also more cookies in general. At lunch. After school. In little plates in the hallways. Way more cookies. Yep, truly a golden age at Finistere. Some kids even whispered that maybe Gale should stay away for a while.

Now that everything else about school was better, we started liking our classes again. Mr. Lofting's class was pretty blissful, animals flying or swinging all around us like we were in some musical about the Garden of Eden, but there was another class that was becoming even more wild and fun.

"Wiki, I've programmed my drone to fly through all of the hoops on the ceiling, but you need to reprogram your robot to catch it at the end. And make sure Emma's programmed that robotic waffle maker to stay on command, because we don't want it knocking down your robot at the end of Lil Droney's maiden voyage." Wiki looked up from his computer and gave me the thumbs-up.

Ms. Love's classroom was like a mad scientist's laboratory, if the scientist lived a hundred years in the future. She had an enormous room full of mechanical contraptions that we could program. There were constantly drones flying above us in every direction, all sizes and shapes of robots bumbling around the classroom, and every desk was on wheels following us around. It was a constant blur of motion that was sometimes dizzying, sometimes made us nervous about a robot revolution, but was mostly the raddest forty-five minutes of our day.

"Ready...launch!" I said, pushing a button and watching my drone fly up from my desk to the super-high ceiling. It flew effortlessly through the first and second hoops, and I started clapping. I wasn't great at coding, so this was a big deal. "You can do it, Lil Droney! Make me proud!" He zoomed toward the faraway third hoop and flew through it quickly. Just one more hoop and he was done. He picked up speed and headed right toward Hoop Four, which was the smallest of the bunch. He was going to make it. He was going to make it. He—no! The drone hit the hoop's edge at high speed and plummeted to the ground, calling out, "Javier, whyyyyyy?" in his robot voice. Ugh. You're C+ at coding too, Javi.

"An excellent attempt," Ms. Love said as she headed over on her drone. She'd added handlebars to a drone that dashed her around the classroom as she hung on, like a personal helicopter or spinning umbrella. "There's just a miniscule mistake in your programming. Wiki, I trust you can fix his little error?" Wiki blushed and nodded. As you probably guessed, Wiki was madly in love with Ms. L. It was inevitable. She was spunky and intense, always inventing awesome new contraptions, and was the smartest person I'd ever met besides Wiki. Brains love brains, I guess.

Wiki looked through my code to figure out where I'd gone wrong, and my attention went to the robotic rice cooker waving awkwardly at me from the floor. "Oh, hey, Shybot 3000," I said, waving back. He ducked behind one of the table's legs, then peeked up and waved again. Shybot was my second favorite robot in the class, after Toastito the robot toaster, which was currently break-dancing in a corner while five kids cheered him on.

"Okay Javi, it was just one line of code. That should do it. Give it a whirl," Wiki said, handing me back the laptop. I pushed the button again and then crossed my fingers tightly. Wiki might have a crush on Ms. L, but every student loved impressing her, me included. My drone flew through all four hoops in a jiffy and then landed in Shybot's little robot arms. "Success!" I yelled, jumping into the air. Toastito looked over and gave me a robot smile and a big thumbs-up.

Ms. L clapped me on the shoulder. "Brilliant work, gentlemen. Now you'll be moving on to the next challenge—programming our robotic vacuum cleaner to conquer a maze." Wiki and I high-fived. On the other side of the classroom, Emma screamed.

"That drone's got my scarf! Ms. Love, help! I'm a Scarfie! I can't lose that scarf!" Ms. L chuckled, gave us a knowing wink, and grabbed on to her drone's handlebars, swooshing over to Emma like a sci-fi Mary Poppins.

A couple of days after Mr. Dragon started, he instituted the Scarfies program. Any student who went out of their way to be kind to another student, did something to better the school, or made an especially awesome project for a class was eligible. Mr. D would walk the halls with these dark red scarves, and when a teacher nominated a student he would wrap the scarf around the student's neck and pronounce them a Scarfie. And being a Scarfie had a lot of benefits. Scarfies could cut the lunch line, take double dessert, and sit wherever they wanted at assemblies, and they didn't need bathroom passes. Teachers also seemed to automatically love a Scarfie and treat them better because they knew they were good humans.

I had to hand it to Mr. D: the Scarfies program worked insanely well. By the end of the week, kids were all holding doors open for each other, volunteering to clean chalkboards, turning in professional-looking science projects, and applauding teachers when they walked into classes. And Mr. D was generous with the scarves. He wasn't handing out one or two a day. Every day I saw more and more students wearing his red scarves in the hall, walking a little taller and smiling. Like I said, it was a golden age at Finistere.

"What's it gonna take for Dragon to gift me a scarf?" Brady pouted at lunch. "I got Rocky to stop bullying Dwight yesterday, my social studies project was immaculate, I skipped recess to clean the entire classroom, and, most important, Mr. D wouldn't even be here if it wasn't for the advice we gave Vlad!" She stamped her foot. "If I don't become a Scarfie by the end of the week, I'm having words with Mr. Vice Principal. He doesn't know who he's messing with."

Of course Brady was obsessed with becoming a Scarfie. One of the side effects of being a nine-year-old ninja warrior is always needing to be the one to win the awards, get the medals, and dominate whatever you're doing. Plus, Brady loved scarves because they were a fashion accessory that you could use as a weapon. She'd watched all sorts of videos about it online.

"I have a feeling you'll be getting scarfed in no time," I said. "And speaking of scarfs, I need to scarf down these little taquitos before they get cold. Taquitooooooooos!"

Taquitos for lunch. How could things possibly get any—

My eyes registered the poster just as I was putting the second taquito into my mouth. There in big red letters were my favorite words in the English language. "Mr. Dragon's Chili Cook-Off!" I practically flew from the lunch table to the wall to read the rest. "Do you have what it takes to impress the dragon? Register now. Cook your heart out. Win a gold medal!" A medal. Even better than a trophy because you can wear it around. Heck, I don't think I'd ever take the thing off.

Brady walked over, noticing I was practically having

a heart attack I was so ecstatic. I pointed excitedly at the words, like I'd forgotten how to read. Then I pointed to the picture of the giant bowl of chili. "I need this. You know my Chili Con Carne Con Chocolate recipe is the best of the best." Then I remembered Reggie, the open-faced abomination, and the crappy third-place trophy I promptly threw in the trash. "Well, I used to be the best of the best, back when I was a great chef."

"You've got this, bro." She looked at the poster and nodded. "Mr. Dragon, how could you be so perfectly perfect?"

Like I said, Golden Age.

9

That night Wiki was over showing me the ins and outs of robotic vacuum cleaner coding when we heard an epic knock on the door. How can a knock on the door be epic? It's hard to put your finger on it, but when someone knocks loudly with the perfect rhythm, it's both booming and polite. I thought there'd be a royal herald waiting at the door, making some grand proclamation—"Hear ye, hear ye!"—so I raced down the stairs to see if he was dressed like a jester. Instead I opened the door to one Mr. Dragon holding an enormous cake in his hands. Huh?

"Javi, hello," he said with a smile and a little bow. (He'd already learned every student's name. The guy was a gem.) "I have a bit of a surprise for your sister. Is she…"

"Mr. Dragon?" Brady glided to the door like she'd just won the lottery. If your goal in school is to be #1 at everything, having the vice principal show up at your house is a dream, not a nightmare. Heck, even I wasn't mad to see Mr. D—he was responsible for everything good happening in our lives. "What a cool surprise! Why are you holding a giant cake?"

"Brady," he said, smiling even more widely, "a little bird told me that you've been distraught about not being a Scarfie yet. However, I have also heard of all your grand accomplishments this week. That kind of behavior deserves a bigger reward than a scarf. I wanted to personally present you with something a bit more… delicious."

Before Brady's head exploded from blushing too intensely, Mami headed over with wide strides. "Este es el Señor Dragón? Ooh, hello Señor Dragón! ¡Que sorpresa! We have heard so many wonderful things about you. Please come in!" Now she was blushing too. She whipped her head back and yelled, "Rodrigo! We have a guest! Ponte el Gilbertito!" In seconds the salsa music was blasting from our speakers. Oh boy, Mom was entering hostess mode. Countdown for this getting awkward—5, 4, 3, 2, 1...

"What a lovely abode you have," Mr. Dragon said as we sat down to feast on the colossal cake. Mom tried to get Wiki to salsa with her as Dad sliced the cake, but he gave her his classic deer-in-a-hundred-headlights look. (Mom kind of terrifies Wiki.)

"Mami, chill!" Brady said through gritted teeth, before turning to the vice principal. "Thanks, Mr. Dragon," she said, her eyes practically hearts. "And thanks for this cake. I think you're the first vice principal in the history of the world to deliver cakes to students' houses."

"Just yours, Brady. This is the only cake I'm delivering."

I got worried that her head was about to explode again.

Sitting two feet away from Mr. D, I realized I'd never taken a close-up look at the guy. He was probably as old as Papi, with skin so white it practically glowed, but the dude had zero wrinkles and teeth that practically glimmered. His long, old-school mustache was an odd choice but maybe a classy touch? Otherwise, I was pretty confident that our vice principal was secretly some model or ex-boy-band member who used to be called the Dragon. Brady put it best later, when she said, "That Dragon's gotta breathe fire because he is smoking hot." And I could tell by Mami's dreamy smile that she thought so too. He had the ladies in the palm of his hand. And Dad and I were cake fiends, so I guess that included us too. Only Wiki wore a skeptical look, but that was Wiki's resting face, so it didn't surprise me much.

"Let's feast!" Dad said as we all dug into our cake. "Mr. Dragon, can we all have a moment of silence for your killer 'stache? That lip foliage is truly next level, and I'm green with jealousy. Can I grow one of those, honey?" Mom gave him her usual "shut it" look and Mr. Dragon couldn't tell if Dad was being serious. I think he hurt Mr. D's feelings! Dad noticed and changed the subject. "Well, we've heard all the legends about your awesomeness, but don't really know much about Finistere's new shining star. Where are you from? Were you a teacher for a long time? Got any fun hobbies?"

For a split second a look of unease crossed Mr. D's

face, but it passed so quickly I bet no one else noticed it. He cleared his throat. "My family is actually from Europe—the Carpathian Mountains, close to the Borgo Pass. I really only moved here a few years ago. I still feel like a bit of an outsider, to be perfectly honest," he said with a sheepish grin. "However, I have been welcomed with open arms by the students and faculty at Finistere, and for that I am eternally grateful. What type of frog is that, by the way?"

It's like he knew the exact right question to ask to get the spotlight all the way off him. Behind Brady was Dad's favorite poster. "The coqui? Oh, my friend..." Dad said, chuckling. "That's Puerto Rico's pride and joy right there. Eleutherodactylus, the most beautiful frog in the galaxy, native to Puerto Rico. They rock you to sleep with the sound of their sonorous call. Co-qui! Co-qui! Well, it sounds more like this." Dad started doing the coqui whistle—low note, super-high note, pause—something he did just about every time a non–Puerto Rican was over for dinner. Everyone rolled their eyes, including Mom, but Mr. D leaned forward and nodded.

"Might I try it?" he asked. Dad nodded, and he

coqui-whistled back to him. They started whistling to each other, Dad teaching him the notes by whistling it over and over as Mr. D repeated it. Then it got weird. Everything got perfectly silent as Dad and Dragon whistled back and forth to each other again and again. All of our eyes went back and forth, to Dad, then Mr. Dragon, then Dad, then Dragon. I felt like I was back in Puerto Rico, lying in a hammock and hearing the tiny frogs sing me a lullaby to sleep. Sleep. Sleep sounded really good at that moment. Just a little nap at the table. Just a teensy little nap...

"Hey!" Wiki clapped loudly, and I shot back awake. Had I fallen asleep? Everyone seemed to jolt awake at the same time and look around. Hadn't Dragon been sitting down a second ago? Brady too. They were both standing at the head of the table.

"No love for coquis, Wiki?" Dad said. "I could listen to them all night."

"As could I," Dragon said. "However, I must head back to my home, as it's getting late. It was lovely meeting you wonderful folk," he said with a dramatic bow.

"But you just got here!" Mom protested. "Stay stay

stay!" She practically tackled him back into his seat, but he kindly sidestepped her and took long strides toward the front door.

"Mr. Dragon!" Wiki said, rushing to another room in the house. "I think you forgot something!" Dragon kept walking toward the door briskly and barely looked back.

"I really must get going. Another enormous huzzah for you, Brady. You can expect a scarf next week when the shipment arrives." Brady's smile practically broke her face. Meanwhile, Wiki rushed back out from—the bathroom?—with Mom's makeup mirror in one hand.

"Mr. Dragon! Mr. Dragon! I think you left this." Had Wiki cracked? He raced to hand it to Mr. D, but our VP was already out the door waving goodbye. When Mr. D glanced back at Wiki he gave the mirror a quick look of revulsion and picked up the pace. Dad closed the door after everyone gave a chorus of dreamy goodbyes, then checked Wiki's forehead temperature.

"Wiki, you're the intense-but-normal one, remember? Javi's the weirdo," he said. "Why exactly are you giving him my wife's mirror?"

Wiki just watched Mr. Dragon walk down the street

in silence, then turned around like he'd seen a ghost. "We're in big trouble, guys." Then he scowled and left. Always a flair for the dramatic, Wiki.

The strangest thing about dinner wasn't the makeup mirror or the coqui lullaby or Wiki's doomsday proclamation. It was the lingering smell of dirt. Not that nice after-rain dirt smell that makes you smile and hug a tree. No, this was a nasty, noxious dirt stink that smelled old and rancid. Did nobody smell it but me? It assaulted my nose until I finally hit the sack.

10

"This is your most annoying Wikism and you
know it, Wiki. You'll just keep up the Mr. Mysterious act
until we beg you to tell us what's got you worried. Well,
not this time," Brady said on the way to school. "I'm
going to ask you once and only once. You're not a fan of
Mr. Dragon all of a sudden, even though he's literally the
greatest human I've ever met. Spill it, bucko. Why?"

Wiki emerged from his personal storm cloud and
shook his head. "Greatest human? You barely even know
the man. Someone gifts you cake and suddenly you're
madly in love?" Brady gave him her deathiest death
stare, and he changed the subject. "Look, the truth is,
I suspect something terrible, but I haven't gathered

enough evidence yet. The pieces are falling into place, though. Once I'm more assured, I'll tell you my thoughts. And if I'm right, we're doomed."

I groaned. This meant he was either going to be wrong but not admit to it, or be right and rub it in our faces for the rest of time. Sometimes being Wiki's friend felt like a lose-lose situation. But being that I was a complete loser, I guess it felt right.

We were about to split ways in the hall when one of Brady's best friends practically threw herself into her arms. "Hey Brady," Amelia said, holding her Scarfies scarf around her mouth, "do you have a bag? I don't feel so great." The three of us gasped a little. Amelia didn't look so great either. Her face looked ash gray, like all the color had been sucked from it and she was in a black-and-white movie. She could barely lift her eyelids, which made it look like she was sleepwalking. And when she talked it sounded a little like she was barfing words onto the scarf. Brady started digging through her backpack while Wiki and I gave her an awkward pat on the back and a "get well soon" and kept walking.

Before first period started, I ducked out to hit the bathroom. I passed the nurse's office and noticed there was a line snaking out of it. How many people were in there? Did someone poison the mashed potatoes? I peeked in and Ms. Nightingale's little office was jam-packed with Scarfies. They all looked just like Amelia: colorless, queasy, and exhausted. I guess it doesn't pay to be a nice person? That seems like a weird moral to the story.

Not a great start to the morning, but at least first period was a riot. It was a presentation day in Ms. Love's class, and the best way to sum it up was a moment where Sally Jenkins was belting out a song while flying around the room on Ms. Love's personal drone, with Toastito clapping and stomping out the rhythm. Coding class wasn't just a learning experience, it was a state of mind. Wiki and I were packing up slowly when Ms. Love approached us.

"Javi, Wiki," she said quietly. "I need to speak with you for a few moments. Not here. Follow me." It felt like being called onstage at a rock concert. Wiki and I mirrored our raised eyebrows and followed her as she power-walked through the middle school and into the high school.

She swerved into a classroom I'd never been inside and beelined to a bookshelf at the far end, glancing behind her shoulder to make sure no one was behind us, then sliding the bookshelf to the side. "Enter, you two," she murmured as she closed the bookshelf door behind us. We were in a tight little corridor lit by a lonely torch that was about to extinguish. Twenty feet away was a thick, wooden door which I pushed open and we walked into...a secret hideout? A medieval teachers' lounge?

The room was wide and everything in it was either stone or wood. There were bookshelves on each wall with books that looked approximately three million years old. In the middle was a big circular table that looked even older than the books.

"Have a seat," Ms. Love said as she took her place at the table. "We shall wait for the others to arrive." After walking around the room once to make sure we hadn't entered a time warp, I did too. Wiki kept pacing nervously. I think he knew what this was about.

"If this is about our amazing new vice principal, all I can say is he's the best. Period. End of story. Next question," Brady said as she walked in with Ahab, Ms. Kahlo, Mr. Lofting, and Mr. Bottom. They all greeted us as they sat down. Ooh, invited to a top secret meeting in a secret room? I should've worn a black suit with sunglasses.

"We shall get to that in a moment," Mr. Bottom told Brady. Then he looked at us. "Hello, Masters Javi and Wiki, and thank you for joining us. The five of us are known by the faculty as the Friends of Gale." He bowed a little. "When the school finds itself in unique and peculiar dilemmas, our council is charged with fixing them."

"Gale has asked us to watch over Finistere in her absence," Ms. Kahlo added. "And, yes, Brady, we did want to ask you a few questions about the new vice principal."

"I knew it!" Wiki said. "I'm not the only one noting the endless red flags."

"Endless mustache, you mean. I can't stomach that preposterous mustache," Ahab growled.

Ms. Kahlo shook her head. "Ahab, you must stop

giving the man such a hard time about that mustache. You're going to give him a complex."

"It's unnatural!" Ahab pointed at us. "You three didn't summon this gent, did you? Use your little table and bell?"

"Of course not," Brady said, and the entire table let out a sigh of relief. "Ms. Vlad told us that he was a friend of someone in the faculty."

Ms. Love scrunched her face up. "We were told the same, but she hasn't mentioned whose friend he is, and she changes the subject whenever we bring it up."

"Then maybe you should drop it," Brady said. "School is the best it's ever been. Just enjoy it and stop worrying."

"Guys, three words: Chili Cook-Off," I said. "Here's two more: extra recess. And let's not forget about the extra cookies. And everyone being nice to each other because of the whole Scarfies program. And did I mention the Chili Cook-Off?"

Wiki stopped pacing and raised up a finger. "We do have one piece of information that might be valuable. An interaction we had with Ms. Vlad." He launched into the story of Ms. Vlad's proposal, though he smartly left out the bit about us accidentally planting an earbud in her office and hearing her cry. He did emphasize the fact that we said no, and that it was literally impossible for Vlad to summon anyone since the bell was locked up. When he was done, Ms. Kahlo let out a deep sigh.

"This just cements my suspicion that something might be amiss," she said, standing up and pacing around the table. "We need to be careful not to jump to conclusions too quickly—Ms. Vlad is an honorable person and friend. Ms. Love, I think you know what to do next." She nodded once. "Children, please tell no one about this meeting or our council. If something does seem suspicious, we will reconvene with you in a few days. Until then, keep your eyes open and report anything that seems off."

Ms. Love escorted us out, closing the secret door behind us. I looked over at Brady, who seemed annoyed, then Wiki. The storm cloud that surrounded his face had gotten darker and way more blustery. If Wiki was the canary in the coal mine, we were all goners.

11

Sunday morning Brady ate her cereal at the window, looking out into the backyard. She ate it slowly, patiently waiting for something. I was in the kitchen, zonked from an eighteen-hour stress-cooking marathon and feeling sorry for myself. The mofongo I'd stayed up late making was C+ mofongo at best, the tostones were in the B– range, and the rice and beans tasted completely off. I really was losing my only talent in life. Why even cook anymore? Maybe I should just throw my chef hat in the fire and get a new passion. Or just watch slime ASMR videos until my mind was fully rotted.

"I'm no chef," I grumbled, plopping my cereal bowl on the table and munching on it gloomily. "I peaked too early. My days of gold medal cooking are over and done with. Forget the cook-off. It's time I retire."

Brady completely ignored me. "Have you heard any weird rumors going around lately, Javi?" She said it quietly while still staring out the window.

"I mean, we do go to Finistere. One kid swears he heard a dragon roar under the floor during gym class. And all the girls in science think Ms. Vlad never sleeps. Of course, both of those are technically true..."

Brady spun around, her lips forming a perfectly flat line. "Luisa Goncalves' sister swears a shape-shifting cat played with her during recess on Friday. I overheard her telling her friends at lunch."

That perked me up. "Oh. That's bad. Really bad. That's gotta be Cheshire."

"She's a first grader, so no one will believe her. But if older kids see the cat..." She squinted her eyes and they got really fiery. "Put on your shoes. We're going to the woods. We need to capture psychokitty before he gets us into trouble."

Well, that snapped me out of my funk. I wasn't about to go prancing around the forest in my pajamas, so I clomped to my room and changed as quickly as a non–morning person can change. Then I headed downstairs and a certain familiar "Hullo Javi!" woke me up like chugging five shots of espresso after gulping ten cups of coffee.

"Kid Mozart!" I ran over to our friend and gave him a big hug, which reminded me how ridiculously itchy his 1700s clothes were. "I should probably scold Brady for using the bell repeatedly, but I'm too psyched to see you again!"

"It has been a while since I've gallivanted in the woods with you and Brady, and I am excited to do so!" he said. "We're here to find that fiendish feline?"

"Before the teachers find him and kill us, yeah. We haven't seen Cheshire since Brady summoned him, so we're guessing he's gotta be in the woods. The spooky, haunted, magical, probably cursed woods. Our chances of success seem pretty...mixed." We laughed.

"Vamos, amigos!" Brady shouted as she came up from the basement. "Into the woods!"

When we opened the front door, Wiki was walking up our walkway, deep in thought. He looked up and his face went from surprise to shock to fury in three milli-seconds. "Wait—what are you thinking? What did the teachers just say?"

"Don't grrr at me, it was Brady! I was changing out of my pj's!" Brady then gave him a look that told him exactly how much she was going to put up with his scolding and he shut up immediately.

"It's good to see you too, Wiki," Kid Mozart said with an easy laugh.

"Sorry, Wolfgang Amadeus. We were just under strict orders not to use the bell. Where are you heading?"

"I lost something in the woods," Brady said, walking quickly. "Now vamonos!" We all did our best to catch up with her.

An hour later we were lost in a section of the woods we weren't super familiar with. Yes, that's an insane statement because we basically grew up in these woods and have probably explored them seven billion times. Of course, we learned pretty recently that these woods weren't exactly the most normal suburban forest. A few things we found out, mostly the hard way:

1. The woods are ridiculously old. Older than any of us can imagine.

2. The woods are pretty infinite. I think parts of them change size and shape all the time.

3. Before Andy was a table, he was the first tree in the forest, and he used to summon historical or fictional people constantly. There were probably unicorns and knights and witches hanging out here back in the day. Must've been a real party.

4. In the past six months we've seen giant spiders, dragons, and insane monsters come out of the woods.

5. We should probably be way more scared of the woods than we are. I blame Brady.

"I hate to be the one to say it, for I'm quite enjoying this afternoon with you, but I for one am growing a bit tired," Mozart said with a smile. "Does anyone else want to head back to your home for some hot chocolate and a symphony from yours truly? I've been working on a new one to play in the Sistine Chapel. I can do it some moderate justice on your piano."

"Amen, Kid M!" I said, attempting to high-five him but getting a blank stare instead. "We can keep looking for him tomorrow. I just bought the ingredients for Mexican hot chocolate and I could get down with some Mozart originals. If it's good enough for the Sistine Chapel, it's probably good enough for our living room." I winked at Kid Mozart, who chuckled. Brady shook her head at me.

"Hmmm," a kiddie-yet-creepy voice said from behind us. "A quartet with no destination, and yet you are so very close to its location. Hee hee hee!"

I don't know which ones of us spun around or screamed, but for a second there it felt like a horror movie. Actually, for at least five seconds to Wiki, because perched on a tree there was our least favorite talking cat head minus a body. And then the head disappeared, leaving only the cat's big smile. And then the smile disappeared, and the whole big, fat cat appeared on a branch even closer to us.

"We're done for!" Wiki screamed, jumping into Brady's arms. She carried him like he was a baby.

"Cat!" Brady yelled. "We need to send you home. Nobody else here can know you exist. You're about to make our lives really difficult with our teachers."

"Nobody makes life difficult for oneself except oneself," the cat said, doing a cartwheel on the branch before disappearing and then reappearing again on Wiki's head. "I am merely here to entertain. Or lead you through this strange terrain." He giggled before going invisible again then popping into existence on another branch.

"Javi," Wiki said as he jumped out of Brady's arms and rubbed the bridge of his nose like he was about to rip it off. "Please tell me this isn't the Cheshire Cat. Please tell me you didn't summon a fictional lunatic creature, breaking Gale's one and only rule."

"Pleased to make your acquaintance, young lord," the cat said. "You have quite the dour disposition. Perhaps I should make your happiness my mission? Try smiling. Like this." He opened his mouth impossibly wide and for a second it felt like we were in that horror movie again.

Brady lunged at the cat, who disappeared and reappeared on a higher branch. "Cheshire! If any other student spots you, this whole jig is up and our teachers will be sent back to their times or worlds. Don't you miss the Mad Hatter and all those folks anyway?"

The cat ignored her, teleported to the ground a few feet away from us, and started walking ahead. After staring at him blankly for a bit, we followed him. (Who doesn't follow a wise-cracking, teleporting cat?) I could tell Wiki was about to explode and let us have it when Cheshire led us through a thick clump of trees to something I thought I'd never see in the woods, or maybe anywhere.

12

We were on the edge of a cliff, which made no sense in this forest, but somehow there was a huge chasm in front of us. A few feet away from me, a thin rope bridge led to the other side. And looming horrifically on the other edge of the chasm, at the top of a windy trail going up a small mountain, was an ancient, abandoned castle.

You'd think that we'd be pretty used to castles, being that we go to Finistere, but this was a very different kind of castle. If you searched "castle" online, you'd probably see a picture of Finistere. But to find this castle, you'd have to search "most trauma-inducing supervillain lairs of all time." If this castle could talk, it'd open its drawbridge mouth and say, "Eeeeeeevil! Eeeeeeevil!" And then probably just eat you alive.

"Let's explore it," said Brady, without skipping a beat. "That clearly doesn't belong in our woods. We have to get to the bottom of this."

She started making her way across the flimsy rope bridge that looked like it was seconds away from snapping in half. Wiki, Mozart, and I looked at each other, and then back at her. Wiki and I yelled some version of "Are you nuts?" and Kid Mozart said, "Cavorting across that jumble gut bridge is lunacy, Brady!" I bet it meant the same thing.

"Are you really going to ignore this monstrosity? It's practically in our backyard!" Brady yelled back, pointing at the castle, which looked more haunted by the second. I shrugged and started across the dental floss bridge. It'd been at least a week since I did something that would likely kill me, and that felt like too long these days. Kid Mozart, being a stand-up dude, followed right after me. "Caution, consider yourself thrown to the wind!" he yelled into the void.

Wiki dug his feet into the ground and crossed his

arms. "You broke the one rule we were supposed to follow and didn't even tell me about it. Count me out. If curiosity kills the cat, take Cheshire with you to certain doom. I'll stay right here." But Cheshire had already disappeared.

By some miracle the bridge held until we'd crossed it, and we made our way up the winding pathway until we got to the drawbridge, which I really, really wished wasn't down. We crossed it quickly (better not to overthink dumb ideas) and dashed into the castle courtyard. Then we had to stop just to take in everything around us.

The castle had seen better days. It had clearly been abandoned for hundreds of years and looked like it might crumble if you leaned on the wrong stone. There were walls all around us, with a few doorways on every side. In the middle there was a well with creepy symbols carved into the edges that looked like a demon portal. And perched on every possible inch of the towers were especially angry ravens cawing threateningly. If I were looking to host a birthday party for a hobgoblin, this would be my first choice.

"Anybody home? If you don't want us exploring your

castle just yell out a simple 'Nah thanks.' We'll head home immediately," I said, then looked at Brady. "Please please don't make us walk into the spooky castle that'll give us all ultra-demented nightmares for life. Please?" I was practically begging her. But we heard absolutely nothing. Actually, it was scarily quiet in that courtyard, and I couldn't decide if heading into the actual castle halls would be worse or better. After a minute of waiting in perfect silence, Brady motioned to us and headed into the closest doorway.

We spent the next few hours exploring the castle. It was absolutely terrifying, and I wanted to come back with a truck full of dynamite to blow it up, but it felt like the evil that once lived in it wasn't around these days. Once we all agreed that it felt very vacant, it was less of a "We're dead!" fear and more of a "Things don't get much spookier than this!" fear. Which was oddly comforting.

Though most of what we saw were ruined rooms, crumbling walls, and cobwebby hallways, we finally stumbled into a big, dark room and froze at its edge. The wind picked up and it whistled through the stones behind us. There's something about hearing the wind in spooky places that reminds me of witches, so I let the crew know that I wasn't moving another inch into whatever torture chamber this was. Brady patted me on the shoulder and walked into the room, Kid Mozart behind her.

"It appears to be a library," Kid Mozart said from the darkness after a few long minutes. "And a large one, even for a castle." Well, if it wasn't a torture chamber, maybe it was a library about torture chambers. "Your eyes do adjust to the darkness, Javi," Kid Mozart said in his oh-so-friendly Mozart way. He and Brady finished searching the room a bit more and then headed up to where I was again. Kid Mozart handed me the dustiest book I'd ever held. "Wiki will want to see this," he said. Good point, though you probably cursed us both, Wolfgang Amadeus. "Can you read it any better than I?" he asked. I flipped through the pages hoping I could, but it definitely wasn't written in English. I shook my head.

"There's one door left," Brady said, pointing past the library hall to an especially dark corridor with a decrepit wooden door at the end of it. "We've been putting it off, but we need to explore it. If something evil lives here, it'd be in the creepiest part of the castle."

"There is nothing alive in this castle except for us," a Caribbean-sounding voice behind us said. We turned around to see a giant spider and all sighed in relief. I know that sounds absurd, but Wiki's aunt turns into a huge arachnid, and we're used to it now. Long story.

"Aunt Nancy! Wow, am I glad to see you," I said, and she morphed into her usual human self. She smiled at us, but it wasn't her usual broad, slightly wicked smile. It was clear that she wasn't a fan of this castle any more than we were. "Actually, if anyone knows this, it's you. Has this castle always been in the woods?" I asked. "I feel like we would've run into it at some point. It's pretty enormous and loud and proud."

She grimaced a little as she looked around. "This castle arrived very recently. I am not sure who it belongs to, but it has been a very long time since something of this size simply appeared in the woods. I do not like it. I will need to consult some friends at Finistere and see if we can come to a conclusion about it. Clearly it is not a good addition to our forest."

Aunt Nancy protected the woods. She was somewhere between a sheriff and a gardener, keeping the forest safe and healthy. I wasn't a fan of seeing her worried because she always seemed impossible to worry. She led us back through the castle, into the courtyard, across the drawbridge, down the path, and across the bridge. Wiki was sitting in front of it reading some book.

"So? Did you find anything else in there?"

"Stinky rooms, crumbly halls, a demon well, and an overall creepiness that should keep us all from sleeping soundly for at least a year," I said. "Oh, and also this." I handed him the dusty book, which looked like it could've turned to ashes in his hand.

He turned the ancient book around in his hands a few times, opened it up to a few different places, and attempted to read it. Then he plopped on the ground and put his head between his knees. He was hyperventilating. I hate when Wiki hyperventilates. It never means good news. "This book is written in Romanian," he said, slightly afraid but supremely furious. "It's in Romanian!" I shrugged and told him I wasn't following.

"That certain doom I predicted? This book means

I'm probably right. If I find one more piece of evidence, we're all as good as dead. Blackbeard was a picnic compared to this."

"Come on children," Aunt Nancy said. "We're gathering the Council tonight. This cannot wait until Monday."

13

Being in school on a weekend feels wrong.
Walking down empty halls you can't help but wonder, who suckered me into coming to school on a Sunday? It's bad enough I have to hang out here five days a week, I don't want to spend my free time looking at smelly lockers and terrible kids' art. That's how I felt until we hit the high school. Then we were walking through an empty castle. That I didn't mind as much.

"Why are we heading to the basement, Aunt Nancy?" Wiki asked. "The Friends of Gale met us in a secret room on the second floor last time."

"We are meeting in the security room. Ms. Love has

a few things she wants to show us." We have a security room at Finistere?

Aunt Nancy took us through a maze of dark hallways until we ended up at a locked door that said "Janitor's Closet." She knocked a long knock with a bizarro rhythm and little robot opened it. Toastito! He proceeded to climb up my body and perch on my shoulder. We walked through a dim corridor, and on the other side was the most memorable security room I'd ever seen.

Instead of a closet-sized room with dinky monitors, it was a vast cave with high ceilings and huge monitors lining the rocky walls. Each one showed a different room or hallway in the school—which was weird because I'd never seen a single security camera at Finistere. Underneath the monitors was a long desk that had keyboards and other electronics that seemed like they were from the future. The room was enormous. It was chock-full of gizmos and gadgets and felt like a superhero team's headquarters. But the first thing I noticed was that it was manned by a bunch of flying monkeys.

"Thank you for contacting us, Aunt Nancy," Ms. Love

said. She was under the biggest monitor in the room and was almost invisible thanks to the flying monkeys surrounding her. She shook Aunt Nancy's hand then nodded seriously at us. "We were actually just hours away from contacting you. Come, there is something you should see." She went to the desk under the big monitor and asked the monkeys to pull stuff up on the screens. They nodded and grunted and started typing on different keyboards or using touch screens on certain monitors. One very familiar winged monkey strutted over to Brady and they began a very over-the-top dance routine.

"While we're waiting," I said, hand raised awkwardly per usual, "can I just ask—why does Finistere need the most epic security system of all time? Is there secretly a ton of crime that happens here?"

There was a laugh behind me, and I turned to see Ms. Kahlo, Mr. Bottom, Mr. Lofting, and Ahab walking in from the door. "Not exactly," Ms. Love said. "The issue at our school is never crime. It's housing so many teachers with secret identities. If any parent or student were to uncover the secret of Finistere, the consequences would be dire. For all of us." Brady gasped, but it might have been because the monkey flung her into the air and caught her.

"I built this system to stay dormant unless someone in the school utters certain keywords," Ms. Love continued. "If someone speaks a keyword, which means they might be onto one of the teachers' identities, the system activates. Thankfully, there hasn't been a big issue for a long time, until the Blackbeard incident. That's when I had to level up the security room." She gave us a playfully mean look. Then she whipped her head around to look at the monitors again. "Now, we've been tracking our vice principal since we last spoke, and we've made an unsettling discovery."

"Please don't be right, please don't be right, please don't be right," I heard Wiki whispering to himself, tensing all of his muscles and half closing his eyes.

"If you were to listen to the audio we've collected, our dear Mr. Dragon is a model citizen," Ms. L said. "He works tirelessly to make this school a better place and is doing a fine job of it. In fact, I've watched his every move at this school and found nothing suspicious."

"I told you!" Brady said. "He's the greatest, end of story. So what's the issue then?"

"Perhaps it is better I show you," Ms. Love said. "My assistants are now running footage of Mr. Dragon on every screen. If everyone could please walk around the monitors and see if anything seems off."

We all started meandering through the room like we were in an art gallery, looking at one monitor, then another. I saw one video of Mr. Jekyll talking to himself, another of a student talking to his imaginary friend, and a really strange one of a ball floating in the air like it was being tossed by an invisible hand. Toastito scratched his toaster head at that one.

"If I may state the obvious," Ahab said in his gruff sailor voice, "none of this footage seems to include our vice principal."

"And that's because..." Ms. Love paused dramatically, "Mr. Dragon does not appear on camera. He is invisible to them."

"Nooooo!" Wiki screamed as he fell to his knees. "Why am I always right? Why? I hate being right lately!" We all jumped and gave Wiki extra room.

"Care to explain yourself there, lad," Ahab said quietly.

Wiki stayed in deflated balloon mode for a while and then finally got up and trudged to the monitors. "Exhibit A," he said, "Mr. D doesn't show up on camera. Or mirrors, I'm guessing." (That explains Wiki's weird mirror incident at our house.) "Exhibit B. Walk a mile in this direction," he pointed his finger toward the woods, "and you'll stumble on an ancient Transylvanian castle." A few teachers gasped. "Exhibit C. This untouched slice of cake." Wiki pulled out a little ziplock with a crumbly slice of the cake Mr. Dragon had given Brady. Had he been carrying that around for days? Ew! "It's the slice Javi's mom served Mr. Dragon when he delivered the cake to Javi's house. He didn't touch it. In fact, he hasn't ever once eaten food while he's been here, I guarantee it." He looked each of us in the eyes, his head moving slowly and intensely. "Do I have to connect the dots for you?"

"There...is a vampire at Finistere," Ms. Kahlo said.

"No," Wiki said darkly, "we already had a vampire here. Ms. Vlad. This isn't just a vampire. This is *the* vampire." He paused one last time, waiting for someone else to say it. When no one did he opened his mouth.

"Our new vice principal is Dracula."

Before any of us had time to faint or scream or spontaneously combust, Aunt Nancy growled, "We need to talk to Vlad."

14

Brady and I ran home to prove that we were
still alive, inhaled our dinner, and told our parents
that we had to head to Wiki's for a stress intervention.
"Wiki's acting a little off, wouldn't you say?" Dad asked
me. "Reminds me of the spring, when you were all acting
strange. Everything okay?" Why did he ask—because
my eye was twitching or because Brady was kickboxing
the couch? I didn't even bother to answer as we sped off
to Aunt Nancy's house.

When we got to the door, Wiki had it opened halfway
and was waiting for us. We walked through all of the
silk tapestries Aunt Nancy had everywhere, holding our
hands in front of us to move them out of the way. Brady

and I still couldn't help staring at her decor, even after coming here millions of times. Aunt Nancy decorated every single wall in the house, meaning that she had paintings and windows on the floors and ceilings of most rooms. Now that we knew she spent part of her life as a humongo spider, her bizarre interior design made more sense, but it was still hard not to stare at it.

Past the long hallway with rooms on either side was the living room, and sitting on her couches were the five members of the Council, Aunt Nancy rocking on her chair and nodding as Ms. Kahlo spoke. When we walked in they all nodded their hellos. Even though we'd just seen them, we were shy for a second—it's so eerie to see your teachers in friends' houses that it shocks the talk out of you.

"She'll be here any second, lads," Ahab said. There was a knock on the door, as if on cue.

"Speak of the devil," Brady said through gritted teeth.

Ms. Vlad walked into the room with the same creepy smile she'd been wearing since Count D showed up.

"Ahab told me something was worrying you. Something that couldn't wait until Monday," she said, with way too much emotion and sensitivity in her voice. Was anyone else completely skeeved out by the new Ms. Vlad?

Ms. Kahlo offered her a spot on a couch, which she took, and Aunt Nancy offered coffee or tea, which she didn't take. "Yes, Dolengen. It seems we've made a most startling discovery, and wanted to ask you your opinion on it," Ms. Kahlo said in a casual, friendly tone. "Nancy, would you like to tell her what you saw?"

Wiki's aunt mentioned the castle, describing it in detail without saying that it was definitely Dracula's. She talked about our afternoon spent exploring its vast and empty halls, the whole time looking carefully at Ms. Vlad's expression, which had gone from smiling to worried to upset. Finally she mentioned the library and handed her the book Brady pilfered.

And then Ms. Vlad started to cry. Now, seeing any adult cry is as awkward as it gets, but seeing a teacher cry is double that, and seeing Ms. Vlad cry is quadruple that, so watching Ms. Vlad's tears stream down her cheeks made me want to jump out of Aunt Nancy's living room window and roll around in her backyard, clawing at my eyes trying to unsee it. As it was, I was covering my eyes with my hands and peeking out between my fingers.

"I'm so very sorry," she said, acting less and less like Ms. Vlad every second. "My intentions were good, but I should have consulted you all. You see, I was overwhelmed and so very lonely." A sob. "The Count is my good friend, and as you have all seen, a brilliant leader. He has such a bad reputation, but he is just wildly misunderstood. I summoned him secretly to prove that he was a good person and I summoned his castle so that he would be comfortable. But I apologize. I shouldn't have used the bell, I should have consulted with the Council, and I feel perfectly awful. I hope you forgive me." Another sob.

Every adult had a different look on their face. For a good thirty seconds nobody could even speak.

"How did you use the bell?" Ms. Kahlo asked quietly. "We'd heard it was safely locked in Gale's cage."

"It should have been," Wiki said, death laser eyes pointed at Brady and me. "But someone thought it'd be a good idea to use it a few times, just for kicks."

The teachers went wide eyed and I pointed at Brady.

"We'll deal with that later," Ahab said. "There's no time to lose. Let's get rid of the castle, send the vampire back immediately, and wait for Principal Gale to decide your fate," he growled. "To the table!"

"One moment, Mr. Thunder," Ms. Kahlo protested. "Clearly it wasn't the right thing to do, but if Ms. Vlad's goal was to prove his worth, I think she has succeeded. The man has done wonders for the school already. I've never seen the students happier or more engaged with their studies. He's a brilliant leader, very kind to the students, and wise beyond his years."

"Beyond his years?" Ahab laughed. "Isn't the man-bat a thousand years old? I for one am not buyin' this charade for one minute. Remember who was oh so very nice to the lot of us last year? That pirate won us all over before tryin' to slaughter us. I don't want to make the same mistake again."

"One may smile, and smile, and be a villain," Mr. Bottom said quietly, and everyone turned to listen. "The only way forward is to have a conversation with him. Dolengen, perhaps you can arrange a meeting with him tomorrow. If his intentions are not pure, we can send him back. If it is clear that he's an honest man, he may stay until Gale's return. We will know the difference."

"My vote is to send him back no matter what he tricks us into believing. Lads," Ahab said, noticing that we were still here. "We've got some teacher business to attend to now. Care to give us some time alone?" We nodded and headed out.

"Javi, the bell is locked up now?" Ms. Kahlo said as she walked us to the door. I nodded. "And we're the only people who know the password?" I nodded again. "Very well. I am trusting you now to keep that bell locked up until Gale's return. Are we clear on that?" A third nod. "The Council will decide what to do with the bell after tonight. Good night." She shut the door behind us.

Wiki's face was so clenched up that it looked like his eyes and mouth had migrated to his nose. For a while he just muttered under his breath as he walked us home. Every third word was *dumb*. Finally he spun to face us and shouted, "Well?" I had no idea what he was talking about so I gave him a dumb shrug. "You do realize that you've jeopardized everyone's lives, right? Do you know anything about Dracula? Here's a fun fact for you—he's literally the most infamous villain of all time. And the most dangerous. Facing down a pirate is one thing. Taking on the king of vampires is something else entirely."

"News flash, Wiki," Brady said. "He's a hero, not a villain. Who cares what he was like before? You heard what Ms. Love said in the security room. He's only been doing good things for Finistere—he hasn't said or done a single bad thing. And they've been watching him. Relax."

"Remind me to bring you some ketchup tomorrow, because you're about to eat those words," Wiki hissed. Then he looked back at me. "There's a lot that doesn't add up here. Tomorrow during lunch and after school we need to hit that library hard. We basically need to inhale every book on Dracula and vampires before heading home. Get some sleep tonight. We're going to need our brains fresh tomorrow."

"You two can nerd out all you want. I don't need to read about Mr. Dragon's past—he's awesome right now and that's all that matters."

"Brady. You're not even a tad suspicious after hearing

that he's the most dangerous man on the planet?" Wiki clearly wanted to retch.

"Welp, we're home," Brady said, pretending to ignore him. "Ta ta for now, Wiki." She smiled her sassiest smile and headed in. All I could do was shrug.

"Sisters, am I right?"

"Library. Tomorrow. Or we're already dead."

I groaned. I hated being already dead.

15

Of course I barely slept, because whenever anyone tells you to sleep well your body plays the prank of not letting you sleep at all. Also, every time I closed my eyes I saw that weird smile on Ms. Vlad's face and got the worst kind of chills. By the time the sun came out I couldn't tell if I'd even slept five minutes, so I wasn't exactly butterflies and rainbows on the walk to school. Wiki was trying to calculate when the Dracula conversation was happening, but I knew it was pointless and ignored him. "What if Dracula doesn't have good intentions and he takes on the teachers?" he asked as we walked into the school. Five teachers and Aunt Nancy versus one vampire? The odds seemed okay to me. But the more I thought about it, the less sure I got, and the more indigestion I felt. I need to stop eating four cheese lasagna for breakfast.

First period was boring, and I did everything I could not to slump my head on my desk and fall asleep. But second period pumped me full of natural caffeine because we had a special visitor.

"Finissons vos essais personnels, classe," Ms. Rouge said. "Please finish your personal essays before we take our vocabulary quiz." I still couldn't believe Mom made me take French this year, when Spanish was the easiest A of all time. (She said something about being trilingual, but I'd rather fill that section of my brain with sushi fusion recipes or mukbang video ideas, thank you very much.) I pulled out my notebook and tried to remember how to say, "Being a C+ Human Being" in French when I heard the door open.

"So wonderful to see you, Mr. Dragon," Ms. Rouge sang, practically curtsying in her all-red getup. My head shot up. In came Mr. D, with his pleasant and oddly warm smile. Any other day I wouldn't have minded a ton, but I was terrified that he'd read my mind somehow and figure out that we were investigating him today. Ms. R was the nicest teacher at Finistere by far, so even if she knew who Dragon really was, she probably would've rolled out the red carpet. "We're just putting the finishing touches on our essais personnels. If you'd like, you can check in with the students. I'm sure some of them would love to share theirs with you. N'est-ce pas vrai, étudiants?" The three kids who actually understood what she'd just said nodded.

"I don't want to interrupt anyone's learning," the Count said. "I'll just take a quiet look while everyone continues writing." He walked down the rows and I tried my hardest to become invisible, though last I checked I didn't have superpowers. Please don't see me. Please don't see me. "Javi, good to see you," he said as I felt his hand on my shoulder. Eep! "Hi. Good. I like things. Things that are good. Good things. Seeing you." I didn't even look up to see his reaction to my garbage sentences. Move along, Dracula. Move along...

"And what, pray tell, is that?" Mr. D asked Mina, who sat across from me and was doodling something at her desk. Whew, saved by the doodler.

"You can't tell? This is Dracula. See the fangs and the big cape and how he's turning into a bat?"

I glanced up and saw Mr. D's eyes go wide for a split second but then he recovered. "Very artistic. He's one of those—what do they call them—vampires, is it?" Well played, Mr. D. "But who is he standing next to?"

Mina looked at him like he was an idiot. "His friends, of course. Duh."

Now Mr. D was confused. "You think that Dracula has friends?" He tried playing down his smile. I guess he found it hilarious that he was lonely and friendless in real life. Yikes.

"Of course Dracula has friends. Don't you ever watch TV or see the old movies? His friends are Frankenstein, Wolfman, the Mummy, the Invisible Guy, and that swamp creature. They're like BFFs. They're always hanging out. That's what makes him the villainiest villain of all time. He's the leader of that monster team. Together they're unstoppable."

He nodded his head a few times before smiling and patting Mina on the shoulder. "That's a fine drawing, young lady. You have a fertile imagination and it pleases me greatly."

Two periods later Wiki and I were jamming food into our mouths as we practically ran to the library. "Okay, I mapped it all out late last night," Wiki said, between chews. "The most important text is obviously *Dracula*, where we'll start. But Bram Stoker also wrote a short story about Dracula, so that will be important too. My guess is that this is the original Dracula, not one of the ones from the hundreds of movie, TV, and book adaptations, because that seems to be Andy's style. So we should focus on the original texts. Apart from that, there are plenty of books and documents that will give us more context on England in the 1890s, vampires throughout history, et cetera. Does that all make sense?"

I nodded vacantly. All I got out of that was: Wiki was going to read *Dracula*, and I was going to read the kid version. "One adult Dracula and one kid's Dracula," I asked Mr. Bottom at the library desk, like I was ordering fast food. Wiki rolled his eyes then explained his approach to Mr. B, who thought it sounded right. He mentioned that the Friends of Gale were meeting with

Mr. Dragon eighth period, then led us over to the S section in fiction. I was surprised by how many versions of *Dracula* we had. Thankfully there was a small version that I could hopefully finish as fast as Wiki's robot brain could finish his Bible-sized one. We brought them over to the sitting area overlooking the stacks, sunk into the big, comfy chairs, and started reading about our vice principal.

The story seemed exactly like I expected it at the beginning. Some rando gets summoned to Castle Dracula, which is super spooky and abandoned, and Dracula treats him pretty nicely for a while, but politely tells him he can't leave just yet. So far the only surprising thing I read was that Dracula had a long, white mustache—never saw that in any of the movies. So this has to be our Mr. D.

As if I summoned him with that thought, who walked into the library that very second but Mr. Batty McBlood-Guzzler himself. I guess I caught his eye—he waved and started heading toward me. Keeping my smile at full blast, I tried to warn Wiki without moving my mouth. "Iki! Iki! Acula! Acula!" Wiki gave me a look and kept reading. I noticed some other book on the desk in front of us, so I dropped my *Dracula* on the floor, picked up the new book, and held it up like it was super interesting.

"Ah Javi, I didn't realize you were *so* enthusiastic about gerbils in cowboy hats." Wait, what book was I holding? "I suppose you must be quite passionate about rodents, to miss recess for this."

I glanced at the book—*Rodent Rodeos: How to Train Your Gerbils to Dress and Act Like Cowboys*. Yeesh. "Um, yep, that's right. Wiki and I are going to get ourselves some gerbils this weekend and I'm super excited to put tiny cowboy hats on them. We're, uh, going to teach them to ride guinea pigs like horses. That'll be cute, right?" I'm not sure I'd ever uttered a stupider sentence in my life, but at least Wiki had time to drop his book to the floor and pick up some other book from the table.

"And this must be your friend Wiki. Pleased to make your acquaintance," he said, with that Dracula charm and politeness. "And what might you be skipping recess to read? *Dorodango: the Japanese Art of Making Mud Dumplings*. Hmm."

Who was sitting at this table before us?

Wiki laughed even more awkwardly than I did. "Um, yes sir, I find mud dumplings, er, fascinating. Who doesn't love mud dumplings?" Dracula gave us a weird look and then excused himself to the stacks. After we were sure we were out of earshot, Wiki turned to me. "You need to spy on him and find out what he's looking up. I bet it's incriminating." Too many syllables, Wiki. I raised an eyebrow. "It'll show us that he's guilty. I'll keep researching, you spy. But please don't get caught. And act casual."

I took a deep breath and walked into the stacks. Almost immediately it felt like being in an ancient labyrinth, since the shelves are fifteen stories high but so dark at the top they seem like they go on to infinity. I listened carefully for footsteps. It sounded like Dracula wasn't far away, so I walked as casually as I could, pretending to look for a book as I got closer. Two aisles down, Dracula was bent over scanning the shelves carefully. I was still far enough away that he wouldn't notice me, so I took a quick glance above him at the sign. He was in the fiction section: Ra–Th. Hmm, that wasn't enough info. I kept pretending to look for a book—I had to wait until he picked an actual book out. I saw his hand move across a shelf—he was definitely looking for a specific book.

Jackpot! He pulled out a medium-sized book with what I think was a red cover. The shelf was two from the bottom, three from the edge. Memorize that, Javi. Drac stood there thumbing through it for a long time, so I snuck over a row so that he wouldn't be able to see me. He was there for a while, probably skimming the book. I looked too weird just standing there, so I picked out the book that was right in front of me and pretended to read it. *The Joys of Fork Bending.* Were there any normal books in this library?

Finally I heard movement and followed the footsteps. He was moving quickly and to a whole other section of the library. I tried to stay one row away from him so he wouldn't see me, but suddenly he walked my way. I had just enough time to lean against the shelf casually and open my book.

"Fork bending? You have very peculiar taste, Javi. Very peculiar."

My heart got stuck in my throat, and the butterflies in my stomach all pulled out their chainsaws. That was too close. Way too close. I breathed deeply a few times and let Dracula get some distance on me. That couldn't happen again or he'd definitely be on to me. Think, Javi. What's a good idea? Standing next to me was Mr. Bottom's ginormous iron ladder, which he used to reach the top shelf. Ooh, that sounds like a thoroughly horrible idea. Yeah, let's try that instead.

I climbed the iron ladder, trying not to clang too much on every rung. By the time I got past the tenth shelf I was getting vertigo, and by the time I got to the top it was practically pitch black. How is this an acceptable high school library? I climbed onto the top of the shelf and crept across it until I got to the other end. Dracula was a few rows away, and I realized that I couldn't see anything. So now I was basically blind and in danger of breaking an arm if I slipped. Bravo, Javi. Another worst idea ever.

But then Dracula doubled back and ended up in the row I was perched over like a gargoyle. Actually, I was kind of perched over it like Dracula. Weird role reversal. Mr. D scanned the shelves for a while, then started pulling out book after book and stacking them in his other arm. This time he walked away quickly, toward the door. I scrambled down the ladder as fast as I could without risking an epic boo-boo and walked quickly to catch up.

By the time I got to Wiki, Dracula was leaving the library. Mr. Bottom looked up just in time to see him leaving with a huge stack of books. "Mr. Dragon, the books need to be checked out! This is a library, after all!" But it was too late, Mr. D was out of earshot. Mr. Bottom shrugged and sat back down.

Wiki looked up from his book. I motioned for him to follow me. First I led him to the fiction area and counted shelves until I found the one missing the book Mr. D snatched. "The first book he took out was a red book from right here..." We looked at the last names in that section of the shelf. Sharp. Shepherd. Shields. "So the author had an Sh- last name."

"Okay, noted. Let's check the other shelves and see if that helps," Wiki said. I led him down row after row until I found the iron ladder again, and then swung to the other side of that shelf. Then I did the math again: if Dracula wasn't bending down or reaching too far up to grab the books, they were probably on the third or fourth shelf. I pointed out the area that I saw him pulling them out. Wiki made a note. "Nonfiction. 398.4. Got it."

We walked back to our table and fell into our chairs. "It's strange," Wiki said. "I was just at 398.4 yesterday. It's the 'paranatural subjects of folklore' section—so basically, vampires and other similar legendary creatures. Is he studying his own kind?"

The recess bell rang and we had to run to class.

Four periods later we were back in the library reading *Dracula*, and I was trying my hardest not to fall asleep. We'd probably been there for an hour when Wiki shot up out of his chair and gave me a super intense look. "Javi, do you know why Dracula travels to London in the book?"

"Are you quizzing me? I didn't think there was going to be a test—I would've taken better notes!"

Wiki read me a line, then flipped to another section and read another line, and did it five more times. He did it so quickly I wasn't following at all. When he looked up and saw my face, he realized I was 100 percent lost. "Dracula clearly goes to England to create an army of vampires. That has to be what he's doing here too."

"You think he's turning kids into vampires?"

"Or the teachers. He needs allies to take over the school. A team."

"A monster team! Earlier today Mina was telling him about the monsters Dracula teams up with in movies. Werewolf guy, the Invisible Man, Frankenstein."

Then Wiki fully jumped out of his seat and stood over me, his eyes practically lasers. "The books he checked out at lunch. He was reading about werewolves and other creatures. And the book he checked out in the fiction section must have been *Frankenstein*, by Mary Shelley." Wiki inhaled all the air in the room. "He's going to force Brady to summon his monster team. He's probably at your house right now."

We made a mad dash for home.

16

"Guys, this is really weird." Brady said it calmly, as if it wasn't strange in the slightest that we practically bashed down the door knocking so hard. When she opened it we fell inside, and she stood looking at us, tapping her nose like she was solving a mystery. "Come on, check this out."

We knew exactly where she was taking us. We sprinted to the dining room, and the mess was even worse than we expected. Half of the chairs were pushed over, there were muddy footprints everywhere, and a slime trail led into the kitchen. One of our bookshelves was completely knocked over, books spilling into the dining room. But what overpowered all of that mess was the absolutely vomitous smell. It smelled like someone had tipped over a fridge full of rotting food and meat, and then a garbage truck had dumped a week's worth of hot garbage on top of it. We held our noses and tried not to hurl as we took in the disaster.

"What exactly happened?" Wiki asked Brady before he kneeled down to look more closely at the mud and slime.

"Nothing happened. That's what's so super weird. Mr. Dragon stopped by to pick up his cake plate. We were chatting on the couches for a little bit, I taught him how to perfect his coqui whistle, and suddenly he just vanished. And then I noticed this."

Wiki got quiet and examined the scene like he was a professional detective. He tested the chairs out, examined the footprints, ran his finger through the slime (ew), smelled it (double ew), and walked around Andy dozens of times. I watched Brady's patience wear down, down, down until finally—

"Wiki! Speak! You know something I don't, but you're doing that thing where you keep it to yourself because you're so dramatic. Just spit it out, bub. I'm tired of waiting."

Wiki stood up calmly, walked over to Brady, and nodded. "When you whistled back and forth to each other like that little frog..."

"Coqui," I said.

"That one. When you did that, did it feel similar to the night Mr. Dragon came with cake and whistled with your dad? Did you feel tired or a little out of it, or like time skipped a beat?"

"Actually, yeah, there was a moment where it felt like I'd hit fast-forward and the shadows jumped."

"Yeah," Wiki said, then let out a long sigh. "What if I told you that you were hypnotized by Dracula, and while you were hypnotized he summoned a crew of infamous monsters to help him with whatever evil plan he's concocted?"

Brady stamped her foot. "I would say that's idiotic. Dracula can't hypnotize people. I'm pretty sure I've watched all the major Dracula movies."

"Read! The! Book! How many times do I have to tell you guys? Read the book. Always read the book. Movies change so much about an original story and the characters, and Andy only summons the original version of fictional characters. So unless you've read the book, you don't know who we're dealing with. The original Dracula, the one you summoned, hypnotizes people. And can control the weather. And I'm sure he can do a ton of other stuff that I haven't read about yet because I'm only a quarter of the way into the novel."

"No! For the last time, Dracula's awesome, and I won't stand for your lies, Wiki."

"Exhibit A: these enormous footprints caked with mud and this overturned bookshelf. Clearly he summoned Frankenstein's monster in this chair. And over here, this trail of slime leading from this overturned chair into the kitchen and out the back door? This is where the swamp monster was summoned. And this piece of bandage left on the floor? This is either from the mummy or the Invisible Man. I'm not sure which one he summoned. Are you really going to ignore this overwhelming evidence?"

"Let's clean this mess up before Mami and Papi get back from work," Brady grunted. Wiki groaned an enormous groan, but we got to work. I'm pretty sure Brady knew Wiki was right, and I was completely convinced, so now the only question was, what next? What do you do when a supervillain invites all of his monster pals to wreak evil on the world?

"Aunt Nancy said the meeting with Dracula went really well," Wiki said, standing over me with a phone. Right, call Aunt Nancy is the first thing you do. "They're absolutely sure he's up to no mischief. I told her what just happened here, and she said that it was impossible, because Dracula was hanging out with the Friends of Gale right now."

"Huh? So how do we explain the slime and mud and bandages?" I asked.

"No idea. I'm going to head home and try to get to the bottom of this. If you two have any epiphanies, call me."

"Sounds good. I know just what to do." Well, I knew the first thing I was going to do. I was going to fix myself a hot pastrami sandwich and eat it in silence. Every hero needs to recharge.

17

I should have realized something was off sooner. First period was Mr. Lofting, but he was nowhere to be found. I didn't even think twice about it, just figured it was a normal case of a teacher being sick. And once you step into a class without a teacher at Finistere, your brain freezes, and your body goes tense.

You know how at normal schools having a sub means everyone's going to act up and have fun and usually just watch a movie? Yeah, that's the opposite of how it goes at Finistere. Especially once you hit seventh grade. Because Finistere's substitute teacher is Conan the Barbarian. And no one acts up in Conan's class. Everyone knows acting up would mean getting ripped in half.

"Does everyone understand the worksheet on CELLS?" Conan barked as he marched slowly down our rows like he was looking for a victim to behead. For some reason Conan always yelled the last word of every sentence. It was a pretty good trick for terrifying us and keeping everyone very, very awake in class. All of us nodded our heads in perfect silence. "Then please take out your pencils and EXECUTE IT." Couldn't he have just said "complete it"?

I glanced up at Conan and started sweating. I guess he was forced to dress like a normal teacher because parents wouldn't love him teaching classes shirtless, but the guy was so ripped that at all times it felt like his bulging muscles would eat his shirt and spit it out of his belly button. And of course he couldn't carry a sword around at school, but that's why he had his yardstick. The dude held it like it was a two-handed sword or huge ax that he was about to swing. Frankly, I'm amazed there hadn't been any Conan-related student casualties yet. Or maybe the school covered them up.

Wiki started wiggling his fingers at me as subtly as he could. When I peeked over it was clear he really wanted to tell me something. Not now, Wiki. Literally pick any other moment in our life except for Conan's class. But he wouldn't stop. Every time Conan wasn't facing us he would try to mouth me something, but I'm the world's worst lip reader. I shook my head and mouthed stop. *Stop.* How did he not take a legendary barbarian's threats seriously? Did he not understand the language of biceps and axes?

Then a note landed on my desk. Wiki! The noise didn't perk Conan's ears, thankfully. I hid the note under my worksheet and kept pretending to understand what cells were all about. Then Wiki started trying to do a little charade and that's when I turned my head so it was obvious I couldn't even see Wiki, and was just laser focused on the worksheet.

And then, just as expected, Conan stopped in front of Wiki. "Is there some kind of problem, William GREEN?" I don't know what Wiki did—if he shook his head, threw his hands up, or shrugged, because looking his way felt like looking at Medusa—but Conan then followed up with, "Come step outside with me, William GREEN. I want to have a word with YOU."

This was it. The moment where Conan mercilessly slaughtered a student. Why did it have to be Wiki? I heard Wiki's weak little footsteps followed by Conan's tree-trunk stomps. Then the door opened and closed and I let out a little yelp. This can't be how it ends. Not because of Wiki's note.

Wiki's note! I unfolded it and read it. "The Council is gone. Many teachers are missing." Wait. What? No. Let's see, obviously Mr. Lofting wasn't here today. And I do remember passing Ahab's class and seeing some other random teacher in there. Ms. Kahlo usually greeted kids in the hall, and we didn't see her today. Still, that was just half of the Council. Unless Wiki passed Ms. Love's room or dipped into the library before school and it was Mr. Bottom-less. (Hah. Bottomless.)

Wiki and Conan walked back in and I breathed a sigh of relief. No murder. Wiki didn't even look terrified. Everything was going to be okay. I ignored him for the rest of class because I didn't want to tempt fate, and just focused on faking my science knowledge until the bell rang. At one point Conan grabbed Lucy's worksheet and yelled, "Don't you understand the function of the

ENDOPLASMIC RETICULUM?" before tearing it in half. Otherwise it was a pretty normal class.

"Were you trying to kill us back there?" I yelled at Wiki as we made our way to second period.

"Did you not read my note? The Council is gone. Other teachers are missing. Today, the day after the teachers confronted Dracula. The day after he summoned his monster crew. Don't you find that more than a little bit suspicious? And extremely alarming?" He shook his head. "I was only seventy-five percent sure, but I asked Conan in the hall and Ms. Love and Mr. Bottom are out today too."

"You dared ask Conan the Barbarian a question? Do you have a death wish?"

Wiki rolled his eyes at me. "Conan's a little rough around the edges and pretty high strung, but he's a hero, Javi. He's not going to do us harm. Sometimes I just wish you'd read a little more."

Sometimes I just wish you'd shut your mouth a little more, Wiki, but I keep that to myself.

Second and third period were normal enough, until Wiki pointed out that we'd seen zero Scarfies all day. I told him they were all probably just home sick, but he said that that was the problem. There was absolutely no normal reason that all the Scarfies would be sick at the same time, when no one else seemed to have what they had. I told him I'd never heard of Dracula making people ill, but then he got a panicked look and said he would lock himself in a bathroom stall until he finished the book. Reading in a bathroom stall—if ever someone wrote a biography of Wiki that should be its title.

18

"**Bro, have you heard who's teaching my class** today?" Brady asked, sprinting toward my lunch table where I was sitting alone because of Toilet Stall Wiki. "You need to skip the beginning of your next class and spend a few minutes in mine. It is absolutely bananas."

"Are you kidding? I can be late to Coding, no problem, but no teacher's going to let me hang out in a fourth grade class. I'll probably get detention or something."

"This teacher's not going to mind at all. He's not even going to notice. Trust me. And Mr. Squirt will blow your mind." Brady practically stuffed my Tater Tots in my mouth until I almost choked and then dragged me to her classroom. I didn't argue anymore, because I did want to see what teacher thought they could get away with a name like Mr. Squirt.

We got to Brady's class a few minutes before the teacher arrived, and I felt pretty weird. Brady told me the desk next to her was empty today (a sick Scarfie, surprise surprise) and practically squeezed me into it herself. A seventh grader sitting in a fourth grade desk surrounded by fourth graders giving me salty looks. Cool cool cool. This was definitely how I wanted to spend my day. After a minute of little kids whispering about me, I told Brady I'd had enough and I'd just peek into her class later.

And then Mr. Squirt walked in. How to describe Mr. Squirt? I could mention that his ears were almost nonexistent, that he had bulging, unblinking eyes, that he didn't seem to have any hair on his body, that his skin was rubbery or that he had webbed fingers. All of that was true, but it was kind of missing the larger point. Because Mr. Squirt was a *fish man*. Half man. Half fish. Picture a mermaid, pretty and graceful and sweet. Now imagine the exact opposite of that. Mr. Squirt is what would happen if you gave a hippo-sized carp human legs and arms and put him in a suit.

How was anyone okay with hiring a fish man for a substitute teacher? Ms. Gale and the Council would be freaking out if they knew! I crossed my fingers that he at least spoke like a gentleman and maybe had convinced the class that he was just a weirdo in a super realistic costume.

"Rrarrwgh! Crrrrarrwgh! Glawwgh rrarrgh! Wgah'nagl fhtagn!" Nope. This guy sounded like he was speaking in farts. Mr. Squirt gesticulated wildly and pointed at the chalkboard at some weird geometric patterns he'd drawn. He hit the chalkboard over and over like he was trying to make a point, but all he was doing was making it wet and slimy. Half of the kids laughed and half of them were crying.

I snuck out as soon as I got the chance. When things seem really bad my brain switches into Spanish mode. "Esto esta horible. Muy horible. Lo peor. Una pesadilla. La peor pesadilla del mundo." Basically, "Everything is bad. Bad bad bad." I didn't need Wiki to tell me that Fish Dude was clearly one of Dracula's monsters, who he thought would make for a decent enough substitute teacher. Suddenly I was questioning Dracula's taste in faculty. And wondering who the other subs were.

I hit the bathroom on the way back to class, and as I washed my hands I heard a familiar voice say, "Well, I finished." I looked into the mirror and watched the stall door slowly swing open behind me. Looking as spooky as I'd ever seen him, feet perched on the toilet lid and arms holding the book, was Wiki Green. "We need to talk." Always a flair for the dramatic, Wiki.

"Yeah, we need to talk," I said, making sure no one else was in the bathroom. "There is a fish monster teaching Brady's class right now. A half-man, half-fish hybrid whose voice sounds like vomit farting. Half-man! Half-fish! All vomit farts!"

Wiki shook his head, unable to process that. "Okay. Wow. Well, I think I know what's happening to the Scarfies. And it's bad. It's really bad. We need to find one so I can be sure. There must be one that was forced to come to school by their parents."

Our first order of business was sneaking Brady out of class. It felt like we were getting to the point where we could really use an action hero, and the Wiki brain plus Javi stomach combo wasn't quite going to cut it. I tapped on the window in her classroom's door and a bunch of kids looked back, some still in terror, some practically rolling on the floor laughing. One of them was Brady. She nodded and calmly walked out of class. Fish Dude didn't seem to notice.

"A Scarfie. Have you seen a Scarfie?" I loved how to the point Wiki always got. Who needs hellos? Brady thought for a minute and then told us to follow her. We fast-walked through the elementary and middle school into the high school. The bell rang just as we were hitting the second floor and Brady was scanning the halls as they filled up with high schoolers.

"Bingo." She pointed straight ahead to a tall guy with glasses who was wearing the signature red scarf and looked like he was about to puke for the seven thousandth time today. Brady and Wiki rushed up to him but I kept my distance. I'm rarely in the mood for a puke shower. Wiki said something to him and pulled his scarf down. Then Wiki reached up and started patting the guy's neck slowly, moving his fingers around it, looking for something. The guy looked as comfortable as someone giving a massage to a cactus.

"Sorry about this," said Wiki. "Actually, could you lean down for a sec?" The guy was too sick to protest. Wiki got close to his neck and scanned it very meticulously. After a few more seconds he looked up at Brady and I. "Drat. Now I'm completely lost."

"Well, you haven't exactly filled us in," Brady said, "So...unless you did that because you're considering a career as a neck masseuse, mind telling us what exactly you're talking about?"

Wiki motioned for me to get closer. The guy was clearly curious too and Wiki would have asked him to leave if he wasn't twice his size. "Okay, I finished the book. The original Dracula didn't bite people once to turn them into vampires. It took multiple bites over days or even weeks, but he'd hypnotize them so they had no idea. The victims would slowly lose their blood and become very sick—and look exactly like all the Scarfies are looking lately." Then he shook his head. "But there's no vampire bite marks on his neck. Dracula always bit victims on the neck. That's why he gave

Scarfies scarves—to cover the bite marks. Or, at least, I thought that was why."

"You mean this?" the high schooler said, pointing to the part of his neck behind his earlobe. "I just noticed it this morning." There in the shadow of his ear, right over a big vein, were two punctures in the skin. Clearly they were bite marks, and they were big enough to be human teeth. Vampire teeth.

"I was right!" Wiki screeched. "Please let me stop being right!" He ran his finger over the bite marks and the high schooler winced. "Sorry about that," he said. "Well, this confirms my worst suspicion. Dracula—" Wiki paused, as if he had just realized that we were in a busy hallway surrounded by students. "Actually, let's go somewhere else. Thanks for letting us know about your bite marks." The sick student looked at us with haunted eyes. I guess he probably thought we'd just given him his death sentence. "Come on Javi. Brady."

19

"**Forget the library,**" Brady said, because she could tell Wiki was leading us that way. "Let's do a walk and talk." Wiki's brain was too overflowing to pay much attention, so he just nodded and kept explaining as Brady led the way.

"So Dracula's ultimate plan in the book is to head to London and create an army of vampires," he said. "Clearly, since that's the Dracula we summoned here, he's got the same plan, and he's starting right in Finistere. The Scarfies were his first batch of vampires, but I'm guessing he's going to try and turn all of us into them. A school full of vampires is a sizeable army. And once he turns someone into a vampire, he can control their minds and make them do his bidding. And, of course, every vampire needs to drink blood, so those vampires turn other people into vampires, and on and on."

"Oh, that's inconvenient," I said, thinking out loud. "The woods will keep Dracula from getting too far, but his little mini-vampires can go wherever they want." The forest had some kind of magic that kept anyone Andy summoned trapped in our general neighborhood. But that rule didn't apply to vampire students. "Wow, did you ever think kid vampires would be the reason the world ended? That's kind of a lame way to go, no?"

"Did you ever think that you and Brady would cause the end of the world?" Wiki said through gritted teeth.

Oh. Right. Six months ago I was an A+ chef who saved the world from pirates. Now I'm a talentless idiot who just caused the end of the world. Great job, Javi. That's some real progress right there.

I glanced over at Wiki. If he knew how to breathe fire he would've burnt me to a crisp. "But there's no time to get angry. Failure is not an option." He took three deep breaths and reset his anger. "Now, what I haven't figured out yet is what Dracula plans to do next. Clearly having that many sick kids is going to alert parents. And he needs to keep feeding on those kids, which means he'll have to break into dozens of houses every night. Honestly, it sounds like a logistical nightmare. And I have no idea what he plans to do with his monsters. Also—" Wiki suddenly stopped and looked around. "Brady, where exactly are you taking us?"

Oh. I'd been so glued into Wiki's rant I hadn't noticed where we were. Which was a practically pitch-black hallway. A few torches. A general feeling of decay and death. Yeah, I knew exactly where we were. And I bet Wiki had figured it out too. Brady had given us a one-way ticket to Ms. Vlad's office. Awesome, we were heading right into the heart of the beast. One of the perks of having an action hero for a sister is being forced to explore the scariest, most dangerous places on the regular. Yee. Haw.

"Think about it," Brady whispered. "Who's the only sane person who could put an end to this right now? Or at least give us some much-needed answers. We need to talk to Ms. Vlad. And I saw Dracula in another classroom a few minutes ago, so I know he's not down here."

I loved when Brady outsmarted and out-planned

Wiki. Watching him realize his brain had been bested was worth a million bucks. It made him a little bit sad and a little bit impressed and he hated to admit when anyone else's plan was a good one. He just nodded his Wiki nod and we made our way through the almost complete dark to Ms. Vlad's office.

"Hello?" Brady said between knocks on her door. "Ms. Vlad?" After a few more knocks, she pushed the door open to an empty office. Well, not entirely empty. There was the weird sacrificial table that made her desk, a couple of uncomfortable-looking chairs, and a coffin. Nope. Two. There were two coffins now. Great.

"Hey, look at that. His-and-hers coffins. How cute," I said. Of course, there was exactly nothing cute about it at all. We walked in and things got way, way less cute when we got body slammed with the stench. It smelled like someone put manure, hot garbage, and rotten eggs in a blender. "Ugh, let's get out of here, before my nose jumps off my face and runs for the hills."

I started walking away, making it a few steps into the dark hallway before I heard voices. At first it was hard to tell whose voices they were, until I heard one very familiar, hard-to-ever-forget voice. "Crrrrarrwgh! Glawwgh rrarrgh!" And soon after that I heard Dracula's Transylvanian bass. And then I realized we were stuck on the other side of a long hallway with no other doors or escape paths in between us. I raced back into the room.

"They're coming! Dracula and his goons! We've got to hide. We've got to—" Scanning the room I realized there was only one hiding place in Ms. Vlad's office. Brady shut the door quietly, shushed us, scanned the room, and made the same realization I did. We all looked at each other, hoping one of us saw absolutely any other option. It was clear no one did. "Into the coffins!" I said as bravely as I could. Brady and I hopped into one of them and Wiki leapt into the other, then shut the top over us. The second I jumped inside, I realized bravery had nothing to do with this. It wasn't scary, it was a new level of disgusting. For some reason, the bottom of the coffin was filled with a few inches of dirt—the stinkiest, most putrescent dirt I will ever smell in my life. The dirt I'd smelled when Mr. Dragon had come over for dinner. "I'm going to hurl. Brady, watch out, I might regurgitate my fish sticks into your hair."

"Shut up and hold it in!" she whisper-yelled. "They're almost here. Come on, if we prop this up a teensy bit we can see what's going on." She pushed the coffin top open the tiniest sliver, and I pushed my face against the opening.

The door opened, and in marched Dracula, Ms. Vlad, Fish Dude, an enormous, freaky-looking guy with weird skin and long black hair, a guy in a trench coat and gloves whose face was completely covered in bandages, and a very normal-looking Asian guy around Papi's age.

"Now for the important question," Dracula said as he closed the door. "Do any of the students suspect you may be more than substitute teachers?"

"I am actually a substitute teacher, remember?" the normal guy said. "Just in a different state. I think the kids might have been suspicious that I wasn't from around here because I kept mentioning my local grocery store. Do you not have any FreshMarts in this town? They're all over San Diego." Who was this guy?

"They were curious about the face surgery I told them I'd had, but they bought it hook, line, and sinker," the bandaged guy said, in a gruff, British voice. "Idiots."

"Hey, I just have to say, you seem way more normal than the mummies I've seen in the movies," normal guy said. "I didn't think you'd speak English or even talk at all, really. Also, you smell way less than I expected."

"For the third time, you gormless dolt, I am not a bloody mummy," the bandaged guy said. "Bandages do not equal mummy."

"You're not fooling anyone," normal guy said. "It's okay if you feel a little old and left out. We're all very nice, welcoming people." The bandaged guy look like he was about to punch him in the face. Dracula groaned.

"Crrrrarrwgh! Glawwgh rrarrgh!" fish dude said, waving his arms frantically. "Rrrargh brargh!"

"I think my aquatic friend is trying to tell us that his students may have been a mite suspicious," the enormous guy said sadly. This guy was putting out serious rain cloud, Eeyore vibes. "I am afraid that my students found me a bit out of the ordinary as well. It is my lot to suffer at their slights. Why? Why must I be so ugly? Such an aberration of nature?" He let out a long sigh.

"Of course they all suspect something. A fish man as a teacher? For a brilliant tactician," Ms. Vlad said to

Dracula, "this was admittedly an extremely stupid part of your plan."

Dracula narrowed his eyes. "Another comment like that and I'll simply mind control you again. I was nice enough to summon the castle and these gents myself. Watch your words or you'll be my puppet once more," he snarled. "And it doesn't matter what the students think, as all the teachers are already hypnotized."

"Please rethink this," Vlad said, desperation in her voice. "It isn't too late to take it back, free the Council, and let us resume normalcy. I wanted to prove everyone wrong, prove to them that you're a good man, Count."

"A man? I am hardly a man, and you are hardly a woman. We are hardly like all the weaklings that surround us at this school. We are vampires. And you said yourself that you're very lonely here. So I am doing you the favor of bringing you company." He smiled a chilling smile. "A lot of company. Enough company to eventually take over the world."

"So what's the next phase of the plan?" the bandaged guy asked. He seemed to be the only guy with half a brain.

"Finally a respectable question. First, I'll command the faculty to gather up the students for an innocent little field trip right to my castle. Then I'll summon a winter storm the likes of which this town has never seen, making it impossible for anyone to reach the school or the castle. We imprison the teachers. And then we begin Project Transformation."

I waited and waited for him to break out into the maniacal laughter that super villains always do after explaining their plan for world domination. No laugh? To be fair, there wasn't anything funny about this situation. At all.

20

"We can't waste a second. This school is about to get impossible to leave, if it isn't already." Wiki spoke breathlessly as we sprinted down the dark hallway.

We'd waited for Dracula and his goons to exit and then waited a little extra time just to be sure. (Anything to avoid getting beat up by a giant fish.) We didn't dare exchange a single word, so my mind was going like a bullet train. Finally Brady couldn't stay still any more so we jumped out of the coffins and dashed through the darkness.

"Usually cutting from the high school into the woods and then following that home is safest," Wiki said, "but now that it's the path toward his castle, I'm not risking it. I think we need to walk calmly but quickly to the elementary school entrance and then beeline it home the normal way. Dracula and his goons will be busy preparing and probably more focused on the woods than the football field. And hopefully the hypnotized teachers aren't looking for us. We should be safe enough."

"Hold on, guys. Hold on," I said as it hit me. "I just realized something devastating." I froze in my tracks. Wiki and Brady practically skidded as they attempted to stop with me. They waited until I could finally unload the dreaded words: "The chili cook-off is off."

"Javi!" Wiki yelled. "Get it together, man!" Brady yanked my arm and we were sprinting again. Did nobody else care about the chili cook-off?

As soon as we hit the normal high school hallways, we tried to keep the perfect pace: the unsuspicious super-fast walk. If it was just me, I could've faked needing to pee really badly, but that doesn't work as well with three people. We worked our way through the high school, then took the long way through the middle and elementary schools that avoided our classes.

As we turned the corner into the second grade hall,

two teachers were coming toward us. Play it cool Javi, play it cool. The closer we got to them, the more noticeable their walk was—it wasn't totally bonkers, but it seemed a little zombie-like. They didn't even notice us as we walked right past them, too involved in their conversation.

"Long white mustaches are definitely coming back. I hear they're all the rage these days," one said to the other.

"Absolutely. They're so dignified and charming. I'm trying to grow one myself," the other said, nodding huge nods. "You know what else is making a comeback? Using dirt as perfume. That soil smell is so earthy and fragrant."

"What was that?" Brady whispered after they'd turned the corner.

"Let's pick up the pace!" Wiki whispered back.

After a couple more scary moments passing a teacher or janitor who was also walking the empty halls, we made it to the front door. We took one last look around for any teachers or monsters, then pushed it open and started running full speed.

"Is there a word for having a trillion questions zooming around your brain but not being able to ask them?" I asked Wiki breathlessly. "Actually, make that two trillion."

"There's no time to debrief. I won't feel safe until we've summoned allies. Now give me a minute to think about who would be the most useful in a time like this," Wiki said, lagging behind because he's not a great runner.

After running through the fields and up the hill we got to the short path next to our house and took a second to catch our breaths. "I shouldn't...have eaten... that quadruple-layer meatball sub...with donuts for bread...for lunch," I said, tasting it in my mouth. Wiki was trying to get us to keep running but was also the tiredest of the three of us, so instead he sank to his knees and tried catching his breath.

Then Brady's hand shot up, pointing into the distance. Wiki and I squinted to see what she was pointing at. Finistere? The football fields? Oh, there was something moving quickly on the field close to the school. Toward us. A big dog? "Puppy! Puppy puppy puppy! I'm gonna name you Cuddles!" Brady squealed, running toward it.

"Brady!" Wiki yelled. "That's not a puppy!" She turned to him as she kept running, giving him a look. "It's Dracula in wolf form."

"Dracula turns into a bat, not a wolf," she yelled. I nodded, surprised Wiki didn't know.

"Brady! The original Dracula turns into a wolf. Don't you, Dracula?" Wiki yelled. Brady stopped and the cute big dog suddenly looked more like an enormous, deadly wolf. Even from this distance I could see his sharp teeth and practically hear his growl. Brady spun around and caught up with us.

"We've only got a minute at most! Run!" Wiki said, and we sprinted as fast as we could down the path. I shoved my key into the door, opened it, and raced into the basement to get the bell. Wiki stayed next to the door.

"Listen carefully," yelled Wiki. "If we make it inside your neighbor's house, we'll be perfectly safe." Huh? "So you need to summon allies as quickly as you can. We need a strong and powerful warrior. And maybe one of our old friends—Hanzo, preferably, since he already knows the situation. Most important of all is a guy named Van Helsing. He's killed Dracula before."

I tried to remember what Wiki said as I yelled the chili cheeseburger password at the cage, took the bell, and raced upstairs. "Javi!" Brady yelled. "There's no time to write the names down. Try to summon them like Gale did, just by telling Andy their names. Go go go go!"

"He's coming down the path!" Wiki screamed. "We only have a few seconds before we're wolf food!"

I jumped into the chair at the head of the table and raised the bell. I knew I had to hurry up and summon people, but my brain was pretty much just screaming WOLF! DEATH! VAMPIRE! MURDER! MEATBALL SUB! DONUTS FOR BREAD! Concentrate, Javi. Just repeat what Wiki said.

"Andy, please summon..." What did Wiki say again? One of our old friends? "Summon Kid Mozart! And also..." Who was the guy who killed Dracula in the book? Bran Belson? Brad Helton? Chad Nelson! "Summon Chad Nelson! And for our third guest..." Summon someone strong and powerful. Think, Javi. When you think strong and powerful, who comes to mind? Got it! "Summon Hercules, baby!" I rang the bell over and over and immediately there was a flash of light and a loud pop.

Sitting at the table was Kid Mozart, some balding, schlubby, middle-aged guy with thick glasses and a dirty button-up shirt, and...a baby with enormous, adult-weightlifter-sized, muscly arms? I was totally confused. But there wasn't a second to waste. Wiki didn't even look toward our guests. He ran to our back door, swung it open, and yelled, "He's here! In the front yard! Come on, everyone out the back! To your neighbor's house!"

Kid Mozart and the balding guy didn't waste a second and sprinted out the door after Wiki and Brady. The baby with the enormous, adult-sized arms looked confused, so I picked him up and ran after them. Just as I was leaving I heard an epic crash coming from the living room. Dracula must have jumped right through the closed window.

My mind got back into its pattern of screaming DEATH DEATH VAMPIRE WOLF DEATH DONUTS MEATBALLS DEATH DEATH DEATH as we opened the side gate, dashed to our neighbor's side door, and thanked the universe that our neighbors never, ever locked their doors. Everyone collapsed into the empty den and Wiki gave a victorious shout. "We made it!"

We heard Cuddles snarl his way through our backyard and make his way toward us. Then Wiki did one of the bravest/stupidest things I've ever seen him do. He opened the side door and waved at wolf Dracula, who was racing right toward him. "Wiki! What are you doing, dummy?" Brady screamed.

"Hi there," Wiki said calmly to wolf Dracula as he bared his teeth and got ready to take the final leap, going right for Wiki's neck. He jumped toward Wiki, I shut both eyes and screamed, and then there was just a calm growl. I opened one eye very slowly. "Oh, do you want to get in here, Dracula? Are you just dying to destroy us all so you can get back to creating your vampire army? Sorry, friendo. You are NOT invited into this house." Wolf Dracula stood there growling, but it was like there was an invisible force field in front of Wiki. Finally after a few loud barks, he turned around and headed back. The last thing I heard was some jingling I couldn't quite place. Then vampire wolf was gone.

"Wiki, you genius moron!" Brady yelled, giving Wiki a big hug that froze him. "How did you manage that?"

"I read the book," he said smugly. "Dracula can't go

inside anyone's home without being invited in. You'd already invited him into your house days ago, but no one had ever invited him into this one. Neat trick, huh?" My head could have exploded at that moment.

"Excellent job, Wiki! I was certain that wolf was going to be the death of us all," Kid Mozart said from behind us. That reminded us that we had guests, and we turned around to meet our powerful allies. Except... They didn't quite look all that powerful.

"Javi..." Wiki said, going from triumphant to super disappointed in less than a second. "Who exactly did you summon?"

"Hey, I'm Chad Nelson," said the balding guy. "I work in IT at a multinational software company. I'm also really into RPG video games and matcha tea."

Wiki gave me a look. "Wiki, this is the guy you asked for. Chad Nelson? He slayed Dracula, remember?" I said.

"I did slay Dracula recently!" Chad said. "He was the final boss in Monster Quest 4. I think I got the high score too. The trick is pushing the B button while you push up-down-down on the controller, which shoots your magic fireball."

Wiki groaned. "Van Helsing. Van Helsing! Not Chad Nelson."

"Well, I am thrilled to be with my fine friends again!" said Kid Mozart. "Wiki, you've looked nothing but disappointed to see me on my last two visits. Perhaps you no longer wish to be friends?"

"Sorry, Kid Mozart, it's not that. I told Javi to invite one of our old friends, meaning Hanzo. There's just a lot of monsters to defeat and people to save. And who is this exactly?" he said, pointing to the baby with freakishly huge arms. "This is the strong hero who's supposed to lead the team, I take it?" He sighed and massaged his temple like he had a brutal headache.

"I told Andy to summon Hercules. I'm not sure how we got this baby bodybuilder exactly..."

"I heard you," Brady said. "You told Andy to summon Hercules, baby. He must have understood Baby Hercules. So this is who we want, just...a baby version."

"Gaa gaa gaa!" said the baby. Then he picked up a chair with one of his huge arms and casually threw it through the closed window.

"Dude! This isn't our house!" I yelled as the glass

shattered loudly. "Look, Wiki, it's no big deal. We can just use the bell again and summon whoever you want."

"Did no one else hear what happened?" Brady said. "Cuddles clearly found the bell in the backyard and took it with him. I heard it jingling for a full minute before it got too far away to hear."

"So this is our epic team, tasked with bringing down the most fearsome monsters in history to rescue a thousand people," Wiki groaned. "Phenomenal."

21

Do you know what failure tastes like? Not little failures, like getting an F on a test or losing a soccer match. I'm talking enormous, catastrophic failures that last a long time and follow you around. Do you know what those taste like? Because I can give you the recipe.

Take a bunch of bread and burn it to a crisp. Then scrape all of that burnt toast onto a moldy, three-hundred-year-old egg. Sprinkle some Casu Marzu on top (that's cheese that's so disgusting it's actually illegal to sell). And finally, dip that monstrosity into a vat of maggots. Now take a huge bite. That's failure.

Well, that's just the first revolting taste. Failure feels different after the shock has worn off. You've got to wait until that burnt, ancient egg with maggots and illegal cheese hits your stomach and you crumple over moaning at your achiest-ever tummy. Now that feeling—a brutal stomachache and nausea that eventually makes you throw up—that's how failure feels to me.

And that's what I was nursing as I quietly snuck out of our neighbor's house and took a walk around the neighborhood. Could Wolf Dracula appear at any moment and devour me? Sure. I didn't even care. Maybe it would be a favor to the world if Javi the Failure turned vampire and mostly hung out in a coffin.

As I walked down the empty road, I ran through my greatest hits. First, I lost a cooking contest that was literally created for me, which was supposed to be an automatic win. Then I decided it would be an awesome idea to summon the world's deadliest villain to our neighborhood—if Vlad hadn't snuck into our house and summoned Dracula, I was about to let her do it anyway. And finally, when I got the chance to save the world from Drac—to summon some heroes who would help our cause—I summoned a ten-year-old pianist, a middle-aged office drone, and a baby.

I wasn't C+ at life. Not even close. I was F– at life. Sure, I got lucky once with Blackbeard and a few good recipes, but now I was pretty much destined to ruin the world. I started looking for the biggest, darkest hole to crawl inside for the next hundred years.

"Your smile looks quite upside down, more like a giant, two-ton frown. Hee hee!"

I practically jumped. There was that nightmare cat with the wild smile, perched on a tree branch above me. "Cheshire! You can't just hang out in this neighborhood. We keep telling you—give away Finistere's secret and the whole school goes down." Then I sighed. "Though, honestly, I don't think it matters anymore. The world is doomed, and it's all my fault."

"My dear, you'll find the world's quite large. Chief Ruiner? I doubt that you're in charge."

I shrugged and shook my head. "No, I definitely ruined it. Give it a few weeks. You'll see. I started a catastrophic mess, and when I was given a chance to fix it, I failed at that too."

"Hmm... You don't appear captured, tied up, or dead. Is it really too late to face the monsters ahead?"

Of course he knew what was going on. Never

underestimate the Cheshire Cat. "You don't get it. We need to face the five deadliest monsters of all time with the lamest team ever. We're so ludicrously outmatched it would be hilarious if it didn't spell out the end of the world. It's hopeless and then some."

"Perhaps I'm wrong, but I've heard some lore that tells me you've saved the world before."

"That was different. We had so many people helping us. The faculty came to our rescue. And Aunt Nancy. And Brady summoned some actual heroes. We had an awesome, kick-butt team."

"You had yourself, and that's enough. No matter the odds, no matter how rough." Cheshire plopped onto my shoulders and I almost fell over. Wow, was he a fat cat. "Now listen carefully and don't be deaf. Use your powers. Become the chef."

I tried to shrug him off my shoulders but he danced around on them playfully. "You know, you're the worst pep-talker ever and your rhymes are giving me a headache. Please please please just go away?"

"The world's fate shifts based on your decisions. So return to your friends and pack provisions."

"Stuff a backpack with some gourmet beef jerky and potato chips? That's your great advice?" I dug my hands into my pockets and walked faster, hoping to lose him. But now he had me thinking about food. And getting hungry.

Fine, Cheshire. I'll go pack snacks. It's going to be a long road ahead, and the last thing I want is us dying with empty stomachs.

22

"Do you guys have any pizza pockets? I had a particularly small breakfast and now I'm just starving. I'm not picky, any flavor's good. Well, I'd prefer pepperoni and anchovies if possible." Chad Nelson was being pretty polite but I was sure Wiki was about to kick him out.

The five of them were sitting in Aunt Nancy's living room. Wiki had brought down his whiteboard and was drawing on it furiously, talking even faster than he drew. Aunt Nancy was nowhere to be found, which is almost never good news, and Wiki was looking stressed. Chad kept interrupting, asking about bathroom breaks and snacks, and he was annoying Wiki as fast as he was winning me over. Clearly this guy had his priorities straight. "Enough, Chad. Enough. Focus. We need to hurry or vampires will take over the world. No time for pizza pockets." Wiki said it as calmly as he could.

I was almost done packing all of the essentials, which I had been prepping for the past half hour in Aunt Nancy's ultra-well-stocked kitchen. One huge baguette with melted garlic and butter. A dozen sorrullitos— little Puerto Rican deep-fried corn sticks—plus gourmet mayoketchup dip. Three Tupperware bowls full of my signature white bean tapenade (a classy baguette spread). A nice little assortment of cheese and meats for a charcuterie plate. And a pineapple ginger sparkler in six separate little thermoses. Were they all restaurant-worthy? Probably not—I was still an awful chef. But it beat starving. I stuffed it all in a big backpack and sat down with the crew.

"The essentials are all packed?" Wiki asked. I nodded professionally. We had all the food we would need, and nothing else seemed all that essential. "Now, is there any part of the castle I haven't mapped out here? I think between the three of us we've got it mostly complete from memory." Brady and I nodded. Castle Dracula looked spooky just scribbled on the whiteboard. I wasn't looking forward to heading over there in person again.

"There's an impenetrable castle. There are teachers inside we have to save. We have to do it without alerting Dracula or his monster crew." Wiki gave us all a serious look. "What we have here is a classic heist situation."

"Yes!" I yelled. "Just like the movies! This is awesome. I want to be the guy who drives the getaway car. Oh, and I want a cool name like Snake Eyes. Well, I don't like snakes. I'm more of a guinea pig guy. Guinea Pig Eyes. Is that a cool last name?" Chad shook his head slowly. "Yeah, you're probably right."

"Ignoring Javi for the moment," Wiki muttered, "let's talk about our heist strategy. We each need to take on a specific role for this to go off without a hitch. I'll take the role of the mastermind. We're going to need someone to take on the role of the coordinator, the gadgets expert, the muscle, the distractor, and potentially the lockpick."

"I'll be the muscle, as usual," Brady said, raising her hand. "Oh, and this guy too, I bet." She pointed at Baby

Hercules, who picked up the coffee table and threw it through the glass door.

"You need to stop doing that," Wiki said through gritted teeth. "Okay, we have the muscle. Any other volunteers for specific roles?"

"I can be the gadget guy," Chad said. "Sometimes I take my pens apart and I make little pen cap shooters with them. I can also make a paper clip jump into the air by bending it a certain way. I'm going to need about thirty minutes to make those gadgets, though."

"I am a fine distractor," Kid Mozart said. "All I require is a piano, preferably a very large one."

"I guess that makes me the lockpick," I said. "I've never picked a lock before but it looks pretty easy in the movies. I bet I can figure it out. I'll probably need a hairpin or a paper clip or something."

"I can make a paper clip into a lockpick," Chad said, raising his hand. "Give me ten minutes. Basically I just need to straighten it out."

Wiki quietly put the dry-erase marker down, calmly stepped out the glass door that Baby Hercules had shattered, walked halfway into Aunt Nancy's backyard, and let out an epic scream. Then he calmly walked back and picked the marker up again.

"We're going to need a different plan," he said.

"We'll need to think of it on the way there," Brady said, jumping off the couch and pointing outside. Storm clouds gathered over the area in fast-forward and it started snowing. Within a minute it went from light snow to a nasty blizzard—thanks a lot, Dracula. We all stood at the window, hypnotized by our impending doom. "Okay, let's go. We might need to improvise, Wiki."

"That might be my least favorite word in the English language," Wiki said.

By the time we entered the woods we were exhausted and mostly frozen. Our cheeks burned, our fingers were icicles, and everyone but Brady agreed that we should give up or wait out the storm. Brady reminded us that the storm wasn't going to let up any time soon if Drac had his way, so it was now or never. We'd all put on layers, heavy coats, and whatever other winter accessories we could find in Aunt Nancy's and our closets. Chad was wearing Papi's winter gear, Kid Mozart had on my old winter coat, and Baby Hercules refused to wear anything. I told the crew that it was pretty inhumane to let a baby walk through a snowstorm wearing only a loincloth, but Wiki reminded me that Hercules was a god. Fair enough.

Once we finally trudged our way through the path next to our house, down the hill, and into the woods, things calmed down a little bit. The trees were still full of leaves, so the snowstorm wasn't as intense in the thick areas. It was the clearings we would have to watch out for, where the snow was piling up already. Brady took the lead, weaving us through the thickest areas of the forest while Chad complained about frostbite, Kid Mozart compared the woods to the snowy forests in Austria, and I got into the intricacies of my open-faced sandwich theory with Wiki, who was clearly ignoring me the whole time.

After hours of trying not to fall over frozen as we pushed on into the woods, we came to an enormous clearing. We would have to cross it to make it to the next part of the woods, but everyone except Brady refused.

"We need to rest and perhaps find a way to build a fire," Kid Mozart said.

"We're done for! Oh we're all done for! What have we done?" Chad moaned as loud as he could. "I knew complaining about my desk job was a bad idea. Why did I make that wish for an adventure? I get that from my video games!"

"Everyone calm down," Brady said. "Yeah, we're all probably an hour away from getting frostbite, and this huge, snowy field isn't going to do any of us any favors. And, yes, this blizzard only seems to get worse every minute. But if we don't push on, everyone we know is going to turn into a vampire. And I don't want to spend the rest of my life dodging vampire bites."

"Guys, if we get turned to vampires, we'll never be hungry for anything except blood," I reminded everyone. "Do you know how disgusting blood tastes? It tastes like cold metal. Nobody likes drinking cold metal. We become vampires and we lose everything. No more tostones. No more mofongo. No more spicy Italian meatball subs." Wait a second. Was I giving the best pep talk of all time? "We need to press on! For the good of triple decker turkey club sandwiches! And the hopes and dreams of sloppy joes everywhere! We must go on! We must—"

Then I collapsed on my face, exhausted and freezing.

My body basically told me to shut my mouth. "Well, this is it Javi," I mumbled into the snow, my face smushed into it. "On the bright side, maybe your body will be frozen and they can put you up in future museums. Here stands an F– chef of the twenty-first century." I could feel myself blacking out. Just a few more seconds...

Whoooooop. I felt my frozen body being lifted into the air and then slung over a shoulder. As I opened my eyes I could only see some kind of deerskin dress and moccasins. And long black hair. This definitely wasn't Chad Nelson. Mystery Woman was walking back into the woods, and as I regained consciousness I noticed that everyone was following her. After a minute or so she grabbed me and put me down, leaning me against a tree. The others were circled around her.

"This unnatural snowstorm emanates from a castle on the other side of these woods. I am guessing that you are all attempting to make it there. Am I correct in that assumption, Javi?"

"You know my name?" She was a kind-looking Native American high-school-aged girl, dressed up like a picture in our history textbook.

"I'm pretty sure I've never met you. Unless you're my fairy godmother," I whispered. Wiki groaned.

"You three have been traveling in these woods for many years. And you are clearly friends of the forest. Your aunt has made that clear to me," the woman said, smiling at Wiki. "I map these woods. It has taken me many years, and it will take me many, many more. You know this forest well enough to understand why." She stood up and offered me her hand, lifting me up too. "Follow me. I will show you a better path to the castle. One that avoids the blizzard."

As she led us deeper into the woods, seemingly in the wrong direction, Brady cleared her throat. I glanced over and she pointed at a coin she had, then at the woman. Then at the coin, then at the woman. "You want to tip her?" I whispered. "Don't you think that would be a little weird?" She rolled her eyes and mouthed, *Forget it*.

After a few minutes, she stopped at a willow tree whose dangly branches were so thick you couldn't see past them. She parted the branches a bit, and inside there was darkness. Brady didn't hesitate for a second and walked inside. I whimpered my way into following her with everyone else. The woman seemed friendly, but this sure looked like a wicked witch's lair.

The willow tree—which I'd never once noticed before in the woods—was enormous, and its two biggest roots jutted out of the ground and framed an entrance to a cave. It looked pitch black in there and we couldn't tell if the cave was five feet deep or five thousand. "Follow this underground passage and it will lead you right to the castle. But please be careful. Your aunt would not want you walking into certain doom."

"Nice to meet you, mystery person," I said, waving awkwardly as I passed her. "Thanks for saving our lives." Everyone else thanked her too, Chad Nelson giving an epic bow and then tripping.

"I am glad we have now officially met. Next time I see you in the woods, we can catch up properly. Good luck in your ventures," she said, disappearing back into the forest.

Brady strutted right into the cave. "Hello?" she said, testing for an echo. But we heard nothing. "Anyone think to bring a flashlight?"

"Your dad keeps a little penlight in his coat," Chad

said. "You could borrow that. I'm going to hang back. In video games the warriors go first and the wizards go last. I'll stay in the middle, where a gadget guy would go. I hope one of you knows how to cast high-level spells." Kid Mozart nodded politely, took the penlight, and joined Brady in the front. At this point anything seemed better than walking through the blizzard, so the rest of us went in after them.

After a while, our eyes got used to the dark, and the tunnel made us ooh and ah. It was a pretty basic tunnel, but there were huge roots coming down from the top like stalactites in jaw-dropping formations. Sometimes they were like curtains that we had to open, and other times they almost looked like rock. For a long time we walked in silence.

"You know who that was, right, guys?" Brady asked.

Wiki nodded. "At least one good thing came of today. We met one of the all-time greats." But no one mentioned who it was, and I was too tired to ask.

We must have walked a half hour at least before Chad piped up. "We've been walking in a dark tunnel for a long time just because some stranger told us to. Does anyone else feel like this might have been a bad idea?" When no one answered, he started talking to himself. "Oh, this is not good, Chaddy. Not good at all. This must be a daydream. Wake up, Chaddy. You're probably asleep on your desk halfway through a spreadsheet. Wake up before you get more drool on the keyboard."

"Who is this guy?" Brady loud-whispered to me. "I thought Andy only summoned people from history and books. He's definitely not historic, and this dude cannot be from a book."

"From a book?" Chad said, right behind us. "I am in a book! Check it out!" Chad whipped a big, floppy book out of his backpack, flipped through it, and pointed to a page proudly. There was a picture of his goofy face with a quote above it: "Shake out your keyboard weekly and the crumbs provide a food diary. You'll remember all the meals you ate at your desk!—Chad Nelson." I flipped to the cover. *Office Etiquette for the Computer Age.* It must have been from thirty years ago. "Handy tip, eh? I'm full of them!"

Brady and I looked at each other, ready to fall on the ground laughing, when a faint light in the distance got our full attention. It became gradually brighter until we emerged from the cave, finding ourselves underneath another willow tree. When we parted the leafy curtains, we could see Drac's castle past a few trees and on the other side of the chasm. And, most important, it wasn't snowing.

"She saved us!" Brady said. "Now I know exactly who I'm doing my next book report about."

With the snow gone and the temperature way warmer than before, we all tossed our coats on the ground and headed to the chasm. Our spirits were high for approximately three minutes before we all slowly made the realization that there was no rope bridge leading to the castle. After looking around for a while, Wiki found the bridge hanging against our side of the chasm.

"Dracula must have cut the bridge!" I said. "Hey Chad, any chance you secretly have superpowers? Maybe the power of flight?"

Chad got very serious. "Do you think I might?" He concentrated, then gave a running start, jumped into the air, and landed hard on his belly. "Nope."

Wiki started mumbling angrily into the chasm, Brady

started punching stuff, and Kid Mozart and I just stood at the edge of the chasm scratching our heads. There had to be some kind of way across. We didn't come all this way just to get stuck here.

Baby Hercules came over, pushed Kid Mozart into one hand, then casually launched him into the air. "Wheeeee!" Mozart screamed, landing in a big pile of leaves on the other side of the chasm. Before I had time to say anything, Baby Hercules launched me into the air too. Aaaaagh! So this is what it felt like to be catapulted! It would have been a lot more fun if I knew I was going to clear the deadly chasm, but before I had time to think about it much, I was in the leaf pile on the other side. Wiki and Brady were high-fiving Baby Hercules (which must have hurt a lot) and then getting catapulted themselves. Chad tried to run away but soon he was screaming his way over too. Finally Baby Hercules took a running start and launched himself over with his muscly arms.

"Baby Hercules! Our hero!" Brady yelled, lifting him up and giving him a huge hug. He gave a little baby giggle, but I was just nervous he'd hug her back. We all thanked Baby Herc and laughed and smiled and spent a good minute being happy and joyful, and then one by one we each slowly turned to look at Castle Drac and watched our happiness get flushed down the toilet.

The castle had been scary enough empty. Knowing that the world's worst monsters were lurking in the hallways ready to destroy us made it tough to summon up the bravado to charge in there. And the blizzard didn't exactly make planning our heist possible.

"Four kids, a baby, and a random guy versus Dracula, Frankenstein, and their monster gang," I said as we all looked up at the looming castle. "We have no weapons, no plan, and we're probably walking into a trap. Oh, and this is Dracula's home turf, so he knows all of the secret passageways and hidden torture chambers. Are we ready to party or what, guys?"

"You left the bell out, ignoring Gale's only rule," Wiki muttered. "Then instead of summoning Hanzo, Van Helsing, and Odin, you brought us this trio." He grabbed me by the shoulders and gave me his laser look. "If we make it through this alive, you owe me a mountain of mofongo and unlimited tostones for life." I nodded meekly, since he would've probably pushed me into the chasm if I argued even the slightest bit.

"The only way is forward," Brady said. "Literally. So let's stop dwelling on the past, calculating our odds, or thinking about open-faced sandwiches. We've got to save the world, and our only option is to save those teachers and take on the monsters together. We've defeated the bad guys before. We can do this. Onward!"

We all charged into the castle, fists raised in the air. It seemed like a good idea at the time...

24

Silence. Isn't it weird how silence can be the most calming thing in the universe, but then at certain times the most terrifying? The six of us stood in the courtyard of Castle Dracula, and there wasn't the slightest peep. Not a little bat squawking. Not the faint sound of someone getting bitten and turned undead. Not even the faraway "muahahahahahah" of a psychotic monster. It was like someone had pushed the mute button on the castle. And it was freaking us out. We stood frozen, all of our backs pressed together, waiting for some sign of life. Nothing. Another minute passed. Still nothing.

"You're the mastermind, Wiki," I whispered.

"Mastermind away. Do we split up? Stick together? Take door number one or door number two?"

"It's too dangerous to split up. Sadly, the only thing standing between us and the monsters is this baby's enormous arms. Let's just hope we can convince him to use them." Baby Herc could sense us all looking at him, and he let out a massive baby burp. Way to inspire confidence, Baby Herc. "The teachers must be imprisoned deep in the castle, so the trick will be getting there without being spotted. Dracula will be expecting us to take the door closest to the gate. Let's take the opposite one. There are also fewer places where they can stage an ambush."

It took Baby Herc carrying Chad over his head to move him, but the rest of us walked single file into door number three, hoping that Dracula's crew had somehow tripped, fallen, and tied themselves up. As we slunk down the silent, barely lit hallways I started wondering if my dream had come true, and they'd be waiting for us as a neatly wrapped bundle begging for mercy.

Then we walked into a small room just to hear the door slam behind us. In the near darkness a slimy voice belched, "Glwarrrgh brarrrgh! Ftagn glwarrgh!" If seeing a fish in a suit was hilarious in a school setting, it was kind of scary in a haunted castle setting. Fish Dude was waving his arms at us as he let out his garbled shout-threats. Chad screamed so loudly and practically in my ear that it freaked me out, and Kid Mozart started gagging, way more grossed out than terrified. But once the shock of a half fish, half man wore off, we realized that he wasn't much of a threat. He was probably just a giant fish wondering how he'd ended up in a full-sized three-piece suit. So instead of being a terrifying showdown, it was more of an awkward standoff. He wasn't going to let us through the door, but he also wasn't going to attack us. I looked over at Baby Herc, hoping he'd do something, but he was fast asleep and snoring like a bear. Suddenly, probably out of boredom, Fish Dude charged us. Okay, now we were scared.

"Bzzzzzrp!" a robotic voice said as something metal and flashy tumbled through the doorway. Toastito rolled into the room in all his robo-toaster glory, doing a few mind-blowing breakdance moves before going into an epic head spin. Fish Dude turned around mid-charge, got confused, and tripped. Toastito kept his attention until Brady and I tied Señor Fish's hands and feet together. Then he glwarrghed and brrrarrrghed.

Brady, Wiki, and I were overjoyed to see Toastito, chanting his name. Our new friends looked confused. Except Chad, who screamed, "This robotic toaster will be the death of us all!" as he ran straight into the wall with a thud.

"Ewww barf," I said, after attempting to help Brady tie up El Fisho. The problem with Fish Bro was that he smelled just like...a giant fish. And I could tell that the slime I was now covered in was going to stick around until I took a long, hot shower. I wonder if Dracula had a shower around here? I wonder if he even had a toilet?

"One down, five to go," Brady said as Toastito high-fived each of us. "Thanks for being a hero." Toastito did his signature robo-thumbs-up and wink.

"Let's keep moving," Wiki said. "Chad, Baby Hercules carried you. Time for you to carry him." Chad awkwardly scooped sleeping Baby Gigundo Arms up and kept his distance from Toastito. Kid Mozart and I took up the rear. Wiki led us down another silent, dark passage that ended up in a huge bedroom. We walked in carefully, making sure there wasn't any ambush coming. In the middle of the room was one of those huge four-poster beds with curtains all around it. Next to it was a rusty suit of armor, the kind you see in movies about olden times.

"Surprise!" a voice yelled, as a guy jumped out from behind the bed curtains. It was the normal guy that Dracula had summoned to be part of his crew. His "surprise!" sounded more like someone throwing a surprise birthday party than a villain threatening us with death. I half expected him to ask us, "Who wants cake?" Who was this guy, anyway?

Chad pushed himself in front of us. "Stand back, guys, I've got this one!" He took a running start, then a big leap. Except, wait, he wasn't leaping toward the guy exactly... He tackled the armor, then started wrestling it on the ground. The guy looked over at us, and we just shrugged as we all watched Chad Nelson fight a regular suit of armor. The weirdest thing was, for most of the fight, the armor was somehow winning. Finally Chad jumped up. "I took down the murderous knight, friends.

Sir Kill-a-lot is no threat to us anymore." Man oh man was this getting too awkward for even me.

"Listen guys," Normal Guy said, walking up to us like he was an old friend. "I have no idea why the vampire summoned me, and I wish I could just go back to being a sub in San Diego. I was teaching a really cool class on porpoises. Anyways, I'm pretty freaked out by the guy, and I need to do what he says so he doesn't turn me undead. I'm supposed to capture all of you, so maybe we just pretend like you guys never walked into this room. Sound good?"

Everyone nodded. "Yeah, that sounds great," I said. "See you later. Good luck getting back to those porpoises." I tapped Chad on the shoulder. "Time to go." He was watching the mannequin like it was going to come to life.

"Team Awesomesauce Squad: 2. Monsters: 0," Chad said as he high-fived himself. Like he had anything to do with it.

25

We were huddled in Dracula's library planning our next move when the books attacked. I'm not kidding. One second Wiki was scribbling a map of the castle on the inside of a dusty old novel and the next a big hardcover hit Chad in the back and he fell over with a yelp. We all swung around and put our backs together, looking frantically for the bad guy who'd thrown the book. The library wasn't especially dark, and our eyes had gotten pretty used to the darkness, so we could see clearly that no one was there. Then three massive, dictionary-sized books threw themselves at Toastito, clanging against his toaster body and knocking him down. We were all petrified, but if anyone was upset it was Baby Hercules, who was probably too young to understand that the impossible was happening. He picked up one of the old couches with one hand and started smashing it around the room like it was a little toy hammer.

Then a dozen books flew from the other side of the room, hitting the rest of us. "Ow ow ow! Ow! Stop it! What did we ever do to you?" I yelled. As if we'd ever been mean to books! "Did Dracula bite you guys? Are you vampire books?" I picked up one of the old tomes to see if it moved. Nope. Just a dusty old book.

Then it got weirder. Chad started floating away. I could tell he was trying to scream, but something was making it sound muffled and garbled. Toastito's programming couldn't make sense of any of this, so he was in full-on freak-out mode, hopping around in circles making dramatic robot noises. "This vampire's house is possessed!" Kid Mozart yelled. "Is everything alive in this castle? Do the couches speak? Do the bureaus attack as well?"

"Nothing's possessed," Wiki grunted, looking frantically in every direction. "It's the Invisible Man! We're powerless against him. I knew he'd be our mightiest foe.

Everyone run in different directions! There's only one of him." We all dashed away taking random routes just to find every door to the library locked. We were trapped! A few seconds after that realization, Brady started floating away from us, biting at the air.

"He's got me! But maybe I can bite him!" The Invisible Man must have been a pro at this villain stuff—she couldn't land a bite or a headbutt. Soon she disappeared. And then, one by one, we all ended up floating away. I was the last one, dreading those invisible hands until suddenly I felt myself grabbed by rough palms and carried over his shoulder.

"Toastito, you're our only hope! Rescue the teachers! Save us all!" I yelled. The robot toaster spun on its head, screaming as smoke came out of his top. I wasn't exactly filled with confidence.

That's when I made the gross realization. "Hey, your clothes aren't invisible, are they?" I said to Invisible Guy as he hauled me away. "That means..." I took a finger and pushed it into where I guessed his back was. I felt cold skin. "You're naked? Ew! You're just walking around Castle Dracula completely in the buff? Put some clothes on, dude! Being invisible isn't worth having to be naked around your friends and family. What if someone can secretly see you like this? Have you ever wondered that?"

But I got no answer. I guess he thought about that a lot and it was a touchy subject. Fair enough.

"We don't know what manner of creature or spirit this is," Kid Mozart said as the invisible hands tossed me into a tiny room with everyone else and shut the door behind me. "If he was really just an invisible person, he would have spoken by now. I haven't heard a word."

"That's because he's smart," said Wiki. "Think about it. How much less scary would you be if you were invisible but you started blabbing away? He knows that silence is terrifying, because nobody knows who he is—or if he's even human. Isn't that true, Invisible Man?" There was no answer. "I know your secret," said Wiki. "You're just a normal person. You're not especially strong or quick; your only advantage is your invisibility."

That gave me an idea. "Guys. Let's play telephone. I'll start." I whispered my plan to Brady, who was next to me. She nodded excitedly and whispered it to Kid Mozart, who told Wiki, and on it went until everyone was in on it. I wondered if this made the Invisible Man nervous. I wondered if he was even in the room with us anymore. Well, we were about to find out.

We spread out across the room. If the Invisible Man was in here with us, he wouldn't know which one of us was about to do what. Then, as quickly as I could, I dug around in my backpack and threw everyone different foods. "Ready...now!" I said. I opened the jelly jar I was holding and threw scoops of it all around me. Wiki took the white bean tapenade and did the same. Kid Mozart and Brady shared the mayoketchup dip, tossing it all around. And Chad went nuts with the chocolate sauce, spraying it in every direction.

For the first few seconds I totally forgot that we were fighting a monster—this was the most fun I'd had with food in a long time! But then Chad's chocolate sauce started floating in the air. "There he is!" Brady yelled. "Pelt him!" Everyone focused their food on the moving blob of chocolate sauce, and soon we could make out a body covered in all sorts of food. Kid Mozart got him in the head good, so there was a big glob of mayoketchup on his face.

"Curse you imbeciles!" the Invisible Man shrieked. "This is the most disgusting solution you could have possibly come up with! For that you will pay. You are still no match for..." But Brady tackled him to the ground and started tying him up.

"Wait," the Invisible Man said as Brady was tightening the knot around his legs. "This is the most delicious dip I've ever had in my life. And this white bean tapenade is just incredible. And the jam—oh the jam! It's like a revelation in my mouth. Oh please don't tie up my arms yet. This heavenly meal is manna from the gods!" Brady ignored him and found his invisible arms. "Wait, let me at least lick my fingers! Please!"

Food from the gods? Heavenly? He didn't sound like he was up to anything. Could my skills have returned? Was I not a C+ chef anymore? Did Javi the Failure get promoted to Javi the Stomach again? I felt like I could fly on wings of mofongo.

"Guys, we're doing it!" I said. "We thought this would be impossible, but so far we've kicked all of these monsters' butts. Maybe we're not the perfect heist team, but we're an unstoppable crew of monster hunters.

We've got it made. There's only one more monster and Dracula, and we're golden!"

"Or maybe no more monsters," a voice said as the door opened. It was Normal Guy, the substitute teacher from San Diego. "Hi again. I was sitting in that room when I realized, I can't stand by while some nice kids get murdered by monsters—what kind of a teacher would I be? Follow me, I know where they're keeping the teachers locked up. Let's finish this."

We all cheered at once. "Victory!" Kid Mozart yelled as we followed the sub out of the room.

26

Normal Guy led us down a few dank hallways
walking on tiptoe, telling us to shush every five seconds
like a field trip bus driver. Finally he stopped in front of
a big open window and peered outside. He motioned to
us and we peeked out with him.

"There it is," he said, pointing to a turret that didn't
seem too far away. "We're almost there. But the only way
to get to that room without alerting the monsters…"
He trailed off, then hopped on the window ledge and
dropped off the side.

"Normal Guy!" I yelled, then we all looked down. He
was on a little ledge a few feet below the window. And
when I say little, I mean teeny—it was barely big enough

to fit his feet. And below that ledge there was an infinite chasm. I couldn't see the bottom—just a million foot drop into nothingness.

"Now we're talking!" said Brady as she hopped out the window like it was nothing. "Come on, scaredy-cats. This is the fun part."

I'm not sure how she convinced Wiki, Chad, or any of us to join her, but two minutes later we were all pushed up against the castle wall trying not to look down at our obvious, horrific deaths. "It's not far," Normal Guy said as we inched along, pointing to a ledge close by.

"I would've rather taken my chances with the monsters," Wiki said, close to fainting.

"Keep it together, Javi. Keep it together," I whispered to myself. Then I started whistling a tune that always calms me down when things get intense. Dad used to play it a lot when we were younger.

"That is beautiful," Kid Mozart said, and he started whistling too, riffing on it. Then Wiki let out a long laugh. Wiki, out of everyone, scuttling on a tiny ledge about to drop into infinity, was chuckling to himself. He'd cracked. He had definitely cracked.

"You're whistling Piano Concerto Number 21," he said. I shrugged as best I could given the circumstances. "You're singing Mozart to Mozart."

Oh. Wow. Then Kid Mozart started laughing, and I started laughing, and Chad Nelson screamed, "Guys! We're all literally about to fall to our deaths! Can you please keep it together?"

"And we're here," Normal Guy said, climbing onto a ledge and then lifting us all up, one after the other. (Except Baby Hercules, of course, who flung himself up.) "It's just across this parapet. I'm pretty sure that's where they have the teachers," he said, pointing to a door across the way.

Wiki asked for a minute to catch his breath, and we realized we all needed a minute—well, maybe three hours, but we didn't have three hours. Above our heavy breathing, I heard an impossible sound. "Brady, do you hear that?" She looked over and shrugged. "It's a coqui. Anyone else hear that whistle?" Wiki, Chad, and Kid Mozart shook their heads. "So I'm officially losing my mind. Cool cool cool."

Normal Guy then looked up at the sky. "Huh.

Interesting. The moon's out so early today. And a full moon at that." He looked over at us casually. "This weird thing happens on full moons. I just black out and have no memory of what happens. The doctors have no idea what it is. I apologize if I just fall down all of a sudden and probably fall asleep or—"

Fall asleep was the last thing he did. All at once he screamed, then he started convulsing. "Everyone, run!" Wiki yelled, realizing something before we did. But we were all frozen in place. I was worried for Normal Guy for a second—he seemed like a nice dude—until I saw his body growing, his clothes ripping, and a ton of hair emerging. He was pulling a Jekyll/Hyde except with way more hair. When his mouth turned into a snout, I had an image that would plague my nightmares for life, and I realized why Dracula had invited this guy to be on his team.

"Werewolf!" I screamed, and the snarling, terrifying nightmare creature ran straight toward me, howling. I had no time to think, so I just put my backpack in front of me like a shield and hid behind it. "Protect me, gourmet picnic foods, protect me!" The werewolf tackled me, raised his hungry jaws, licked his wolf lips and feasted on my head. No, not my head—my backpack? The charcuterie! He ripped open my backpack and was eating all the delicious meats Aunt Nancy had stocked in her fridge. "That mortadella is delicious, right, boy?" I said, laughing nervously. "Aunt Nancy buys it from a really fancy place that sells only to restaurants."

The werewolf ate and ate—I guess I did pack a lot of charcuterie—and I started calming down. It was kind of funny having a werewolf chow down on fancy deli meats. It almost tickled me, the way he was rubbing his snout against my tummy while he ate. This wasn't so bad at all. Then he stopped, looked around my backpack, and realized there was no more charcuterie left. Now he was eyeing my face. Oh no. Adios, everyone! It was nice knowing you! His horror snout flared up, his mouth drooled, and his breath smelled like bologna. This was no way to go. Then he struck at me, right at my face. It was like time froze. His mouth opened impossibly wide, like it was going to bite off my whole head. It got closer and closer until I could see his nasty tonsils. Bye-bye life.

"Hey! Hey boy!" Brady whistled behind me. The werewolf's head shot up to look. Brady stepped closer to Wolfy, super calm, as if he wasn't about to devour us all. She held up her hand firmly. "I didn't say you could eat my brother." Huh? She snapped a few times and pointed at the floor. Werewolf climbed off me and walked over to her on all fours, snarling a little bit. "Look at me. Right here. Look at me." She pointed with two fingers at her eyes. Werewolf stopped snarling, looking more curious than anything else. "Who's the pack leader? Who's the alpha dog here?" He yelped a little. Then her voice got icy. "I am. I am always the alpha. Always."

Werewolf started whining and put his tail between his legs.

"Good doggie. You're a very good doggie." She petted the werewolf a little bit. "Now...scram!" she yelled, pointing behind us. And the werewolf took off at full speed on all fours.

Brady offered me her hand and yanked me up, still in ninja warrior mode. "You're welcome. Let's go."

27

We made our way across the parapet, down some stairs, and to a heavy wooden door with a massive ancient lock. Brady immediately started roundhouse kicking it until Baby Hercules realized what she was doing and lazily tore the door out of the frame, throwing it into the endless chasm. "Never leave home without a Baby Hercules," I muttered.

Inside was a large room barely lit by torches, packed with people. "It appears we've found your educators!" Kid Mozart said as we stepped into the room, our eyes adjusting to the darkness. Hmm... These dark blobs looked too short to be teachers. Students? Oh wait.

"Scarfies!" Brady yelled, getting into a kung fu stance.

But instead of attacking us or charging at our throats, the Scarfies just walked around, a few talking to each other, looking super bored. They barely even noticed that we were there.

"Um, Scarfies? Hello? Anyone home?" I asked as the six of us walked into the crowd carefully. I looked around for a Scarfie I recognized. Oh no. Not him. Not Mr. First Place Champion, Señor Open Faced Scandinavian Shrimp Sandwich himself. Reggie Donaldson, my culinary arch nemesis. Wiki noticed him approaching me and grimaced. I braced myself for a painful conversation. "Don't get into your open-faced sandwich theory. Don't do it," I whispered to myself.

"Hey Javi, I've been wanting to ask you something," he said quietly. This was going to be bad...

"Don't you love the way Mr. Dragon smells?" Um... what? "That earthy aroma is so organic. Pungent in the best way. We've been rubbing dirt in our hair to try to get the same fragrance." Excuse me? He looked like he was half-asleep. Then he came in close and studied my upper lip. "Hmm, it's going to be a while until you get some growth there, but at least you can technically grow a mustache. I'm still working on a nice, long, white mustache of my own. Maybe we'll be mustache brothers soon."

When I looked around to see if anyone else was hearing this nonsense, I noticed that a bunch of Scarfies were gathering around each other's pocket mirrors and studying their chins and upper lips. "You've got a lot of space between your nose and your lips. You could grow a bushy, white beauty of a mustache there," I heard one kid say. "How's mine coming in? It'll never be as classy as Mr. Dragon's, but at least I can dream."

"They're all hypnotized," Wiki said. "But Dracula isn't commanding them to do anything at the moment, so they're just milling about waiting for an order."

"Excuse me, friends," Kid Mozart squeaked. "This is very abnormal." He was surrounded by Scarfies petting his white wig and studying it carefully.

"How did you get your hair so perfectly white? Tell us your secret," one said dreamily. Reggie Donaldson gazed at Mozart lovingly as he ate some kind of candy he was holding in his cupped hand.

"Want one?" he asked, offering me a piece. At first I

thought he'd cooked something that bested my great-est desserts and was rubbing it in. Nope. There was a grubby, grimy centipede wriggling between his fingers. "No?" He popped it in his mouth and munched on it slowly. EW. His other hand was filled with live insects crawling around waiting to be eaten. What had become of my arch nemesis? I actually felt sorry for the guy!

"Guys, let's get out of here," I said. "This is creeping me out. And we've got to find the teachers." As I looked around I realized someone was missing. "Chad? Where'd you go?"

Chad emerged from the crowd shuffling toward us like a zombie with two bright red bite marks on his neck. "Some of the Scarfies have turned to vampires already!" Wiki shouted. Brady, Wiki, and I practically magnetized to each other as we walked backward slowly, eyeing the crowd of Scarfies for full-on vampires. "Oh no, not you Kid Mozart," Wiki groaned. I looked over and there was little Wolfgang Amadeus, his wig falling halfway off his head, blood dripping down his neck from the big vampire bite marks. And Baby Hercules was nowhere to be seen.

Before I could react, our backs hit up against a wall. Hmm, this wall felt fleshier than it should. I looked up at the shadow looming above us. Yeah, this wasn't a wall at all.

"Monster!" Wiki screamed as a huge hand scooped us all up and carried us away. The last thing I heard was the sound of a coqui. I guess my brain and my body were racing to see which one would crack first.

28

"Hey!" Brady said. "You don't just snatch people in the dark like that! What kind of a monster are you?"

"Frankestein's monster," he said calmly. "That is the monster that I am. The vampire requires you three," he said in his husky voice as he walked with huge monster strides. "It appears that you might be able to hasten his malevolent plans."

"Hasten? Malevolent plans? Aren't you supposed to talk like 'Me Frankenstein, you dead?' You sound more like Shakespeare than Frankenstein," Brady said. Frankenstein wasn't too happy to hear that, and he squeezed us harder.

"Brady," Wiki gasped, "I'm not going to say it again.

Read. The. Book. The movie version of Frankenstein's monster is nothing like the original one. He speaks eloquently. He has long hair. He isn't even necessarily a villain; he becomes one because everyone treats him like a monster." I felt a drop of water fall on my neck. Rain? A leak? Or did Frankenstein just shed a tear?

"We have arrived," he said, walking toward two big doors and swinging one open. I don't know who gasped loudest, but the three of us did it at the exact same time.

We were in a huge room that must have been used for feasts and parties before Dracula went vampirey. There was a big fireplace at one end, thick wooden tables that had been moved to the edges, and some massive torch-filled chandeliers hung from the high stone ceiling. In the middle of the room were maybe fifty Finistere students all standing still and in a daze. Sitting above them, on a black throne, was Drac himself, with the evilest smile imaginable dancing on his self-satisfied face. Ms. Vlad was at his side, her eyes half-lidded, deep in a trance.

Wait. Why was King Vampiro looking decades younger? "Psst! Did Dracula get a makeover? Plastic surgery? His hair is jet black and the dude looks like he just graduated high school."

"It's because he's been feasting on human blood. He ages in reverse when he drinks our blood," Wiki whispered back.

File that under: questions I should have never, ever asked.

"My honored guests!" Dracula said, standing up as he saw us, smiling his biggest vampire smile. "I am so happy you have joined us. I wanted to thank you sincerely for allowing Vlad to bring me to your lovely school." He walked toward us, and I felt the hairs on my neck raise up—then detach and run away screaming. "To think that I was going to attempt to raise a vampire army in London, when this is a thousand times easier. Now, to thank you for this gift you have bestowed on me, I want to make you the generals of my army. But first, to begin the transformation." He bared his fangs. I pushed my head into my shoulders, hoping I could turn into a turtle. Go away, you pesky neck, go away.

"We trusted you, and now you do this? How dare you?" Brady spat. "You really are a monster."

"Dear child," Dracula said, pretending to be innocently offended, "I am giving you and your schoolmates the greatest gift of all. Eternal life. You will live forever, like me."

"Don't follow me," Brady whispered to Wiki and me. "I have an idea." She bit Frankenstein's hand. He grunted and dropped us, then Brady dashed back to where we came from, yelling, "Catch me if you can, Frankie!"

Dracula looked only mildly annoyed. "Get the girl," he said to the monster, who nodded and ran after her. Given that he was three times her size, I was pretty sure it'd take him all of fifteen seconds to catch her. Great plan, Brady. Great plan.

"Eternal life sounds great," Wiki said, walking closer to Drac, "but I read all about how it works, and it's awful. You're always thirsty, you sleep in a smelly coffin filled with old dirt, you live in a disgusting, abandoned castle, you have no friends, and you hate the daytime. Sounds like a terrible way to live."

Dracula's smile vanished, and his eyes got very narrow as he approached Wiki. "William Green. The boy who reads too much." He was two feet away from

Wiki, and I started to panic. Why wasn't Wiki running away? "If you know me so well, perhaps you know of my strength? And my speed?"

"Y-you have the strength of t-t-twenty men," Wiki stammered, realizing that his bravado might not have been the smartest strategy in the world. "And you're extremely agile."

"True on both counts," Dracula said. Then he moved so quickly all I saw was a blur. When my eyes could focus again, Wiki was limp in the vampire's arms, and Dracula had sunk his fangs into his neck. Wiki fainted, and Dracula let him drop to the floor.

"Wiki!" I screamed. He wasn't moving.

"He is fine, I assure you," Dracula said calmly. "Better than fine. He has been blessed. As has your sister."

What? He must have read my confusion from all the way across the room.

"When I hypnotized her at your house, I took the liberty of beginning her transformation. She will soon be blessed with eternal life as well. You're welcome."

Anger and terror were having a boxing match in my brain. I looked around frantically for allies—someone, anyone, to help me.

"Are you seeking your teacher friends? I can fetch them for you," Dracula said with his terrible smile. He snapped and a parade of faculty came zombie-walking out of a side door into the hallway. At least two of them were talking up white mustaches. "You see, you're the last one, Javi. The Scarfies that have fully turned vampire have bitten the rest of the students. It looks like you're the only one left." Seeing the Friends of Gale and Aunt Nancy zombified was the last straw. I did what any brave person in my situation would do.

I ran. "Bye!" I yelled for some reason as I turned around and tore out of the room...right into the Scarfies, who were parading back in.

"Bring him here," Dracula said firmly, and the Scarfies switched from bored mode into killer robot mode. The two closest to me grabbed me by the arms and lifted me above their heads, passing me to the next Scarfies, and then those passed me to the next. Were they crowd-surfing me to Dracula? I felt like I was in the most intense death metal concert of my life. But also I was panicking like never before.

Then I caught sight of it. Perched on the top of Dracula's throne was Eleutherodactylus himself—a coquí! So Dracula summoned the worst monsters in history...and a Puerto Rican frog? What a weirdo. Must have fallen in love with its song. The song that was calming me down and reminding me of Puerto Rican beaches. Of salsa music. Of delicious mofongo with olive oil and—

Wait. That gave me an idea. Oh, wow, was it really dumb, but also vaguely awesome. Okay, how to put this plan into action... Too little, too late, Javi—these Scarfies are basically feeding you to Dracula. I peered down and saw the vampire getting closer and closer.

"Let the creation of Dracula's Army begin!" he said, baring his fangs again.

"No!" Ms. Vlad yelled, snapping out of her daze and holding onto his hand. "You can still stop, Count. It isn't too late. Don't do this. Don't betray those of us who brought you here, who believed you could be a good person."

"For the last time," Drac said, shrugging her off, "I am not a person anymore. Neither are you. We are vampires. We need more of our kind here with us." He looked at her with murderous eyes. "In fact, maybe I should force you to create our army instead. How amusing would the headline be? Principal bites students, turns school into vampires. Perhaps I should have you do this."

"No! Please, no! Stop!" Dracula turned around and his eyes locked onto mine. I only had a few seconds before I went fangy too. Distraction? Can I get a teensy distraction please? Anyone?

"The cavalry has arrived!" a very familiar voice cawed. I looked over and flying in through the window was Polynesia, the parrot, with all of Mr. Lofting's other pets following her. They headed straight for the Scarfies. Vampire kids versus hyperintelligent animals—this was as weird as it gets. Wait, no it wasn't. Two seconds later Toastito flew in through the window riding a minicopter, followed by an army of drones.

"You did it, Toastito! I knew you could do it!" I yelled. Toastito gave me the peace sign with his biggest robosmile yet.

The drones and animals squared off against the Scarfies, mostly just annoying them and getting in their hair. (Except Dab-Dab, who was kicking butt and taking names.) That was the only distraction I needed.

I reached into my backpack and pulled out my epic sword. Well, my epic sword-like baguette. Yes, the fate of the world was on my shoulders, I had to save the planet from going vampire, and my brilliant/horrible plan was attacking the world's most powerful monster with a big loaf of bread.

There was a 99 percent chance this was the dumbest idea of all time and a 1 percent chance this was genius. Hey, why not?

I pulled the loaf from my backpack and held it like a two-handed sword, trying to channel Conan's energy. "Beware, Dracula. I have an artisanal baguette and I know how to use it!" I swung toward him a few times, and he stopped. He looked at the bread and looked at me with eyes that said, Are you being serious right now? You're attacking me with a loaf of bread? But it was too late to back down, so I rushed at him with my baguette raised behind me.

"You could've had a nice, comfy life at Finistere. You could've been a legendary principal. You could've gotten unlimited love from Brady and the rest of the students and we wouldn't have even questioned your demented mustache. But instead you lied to us and betrayed us. And that's not the worst part. You tried to win me over with that chili cook-off. A chili cook-off you could have never judged fairly. You know why? Vampires! Don't! Eat!"

I swung the baguette like a baseball bat at him. What should have happened next—the bread breaking, Dracula laughing as he lifted me up with one hand, bit me, and turned me into a vampire—didn't happen.

When the bread hit Dracula, he screamed. Wow, could this actually work? I kept swinging at him with the baguette, and he shrank down. "No! Spare me! Please!" Then I took a chunk of the bread off and pushed it in his face. "Aaagh, stop! Anything but this! It burns! It burns! You win! I surrender! You win!"

We win? Did I just single-handedly defeat Dracula?? I felt the thrill of victory rush through my body. If failure tasted like moldy, maggoty bread, then success tasted like a cotton candy burrito stuffed with coconut ice cream plus all the fixings. (Or Puerto Rican Mallorca. Google it.) We won! We Won! I...am standing here with a piece of bread smushed in Dracula's face and things are getting really awkward... What now?

Frankenstein busted through the door and charged straight toward me. Oh right. Frankenstein. If there was one life lesson I would take away from this, it was never forget about Frankenstein. But of course, I wouldn't take any life lessons away from this because I was five seconds away from getting murdered! The enormous ogre-dude sprinted across the room and jumped up the stairs, and his huge hand swiped right at my face.

Not my face? He picked up Dracula, taking my bread and keeping it firmly shoved in his face. "Come," he said to me. "We must take this one back to the table and send him back to his home."

Then I noticed Brady riding on his back. "Go Team Frankenstein!" she yelled, giving me the thumbs-up.

"I prefer we dub our duo Team Brady," a smiling Frankenstein said. "Or perhaps we combine names. Team Brankenstein?" Did Frankenstein just make a joke?

Frankenstein threw Dracula over his shoulder and motioned for me to join him. "The vampire must go back. Then everyone returns to normal."

"But what if he succeeds in taking over the world back then?"

Frankenstein smiled at me. "Have you read the book?"

29

"Could everyone assemble in the cafeteria, please? Everyone assemble in the cafeteria." The announcement blared as Brady and I walked back into school after Mission: Adios Vampiro. We shrugged and headed to the cafeteria that the middle school and elementary shared.

The slog back home with Dracula took forever, but he passed out pretty soon after Frankenstein started carrying him, so we got to spend the rest of the time getting to know my new favorite monster. It turns out that Brady's plan was simple and genius. She could tell that Frankie wasn't evil—just sad and misunderstood. All he ever wanted in life was a hug. So when she gave him a huge, five-minute Brady-hug, they instantly became friends for life, and he became our personal hero.

Frankenstein told us his story, and I've got to admit, it's super sad. Brady told him not to worry, that he didn't have to go back to his horror show world and keep getting bullied. We just needed to figure out the right angle to sell him to Principal Gale. If she could find a place for him on the faculty, she'd do it. It would've been easier if Frankie wasn't eight feet tall with glowing eyes, black lips, and almost transparent yellow skin. We spent the whole walk back brainstorming, and even though we didn't come up with any winning ideas yet, we told him to sit tight. We'd figure something out.

We woke up Dracula right before we sent him off, just to yell at him a little bit. He reminded us of all the cookies and recess he gave us while he was vice principal, and that ultimately he was giving us the gift of eternal life. He asked if we wanted him to turn into his cute puppy self again, and Brady almost took him up on it, so I rang the bell. Vamoose, vampire.

"Hey, what's going to happen to Finistere now?" I asked Brady as we walked into the cafeteria. "Everything today has been so nutso. I just realized that every teacher's cover is blown. Every student in this school was just taken to Dracula's castle, some of them were bitten and hypnotized, most of them saw Ms. Vlad in vampire mode, and who knows what else they saw. This doesn't exactly bode well for the future of the school. Especially with Gale being absent."

Brady froze. Yep, she hadn't thought about it either. "This is bad, Javi. This is almost as bad as the whole Dracula fiasco. They're going to send all the teachers back to their own worlds. And then they'll probably ship Andy off to some lab where they'll force him to summon people nonstop. This school's going to shut down. We're going to be sent to a boring old normal school." Every sentence got faster and faster until she got quiet and I could tell the sentences were going faster and faster in her head.

"Lad. Lass." Captain Ahab put a friendly hand on our shoulders. "Ye'll be wanting to meet us in the Council chamber after this little meal. Don't delay. There's a lot to debrief on." Then he smiled and slapped us on the back. "You've got a real knack for getting us out of some serious pickles, you know that? I would've promoted either of ye to first mate if we were on the *Pequod*." He started walking away, then turned around and whispered, "Don't eat the soup. Do *not* eat the soup."

Soup? "Did you notice how relaxed he was?" I asked Brady. "Maybe they've got a plan?"

"What plan could you even have?" Brady asked. "Make every single student pinky swear that they won't tell their parents that they were captured by an ancient vampire and taken to his evil castle? Yeah, good luck with that."

An old, squat Asian woman walked in front of us holding a huge pot of soup. When she passed us, she looked up and winked. She had a very Aunt Nancy–esque smile—sly and maybe a little wicked. "Meng Po," Ms. Kahlo called out. "Bring it over here." She nodded and waddled the soup over.

"All right, lads and lasses, all of ye sit down and listen," Ahab said, standing on a table. "We've all been through a lot today. We've seen things that seemed impossible. We've encountered terrifying creatures that shouldn't exist. Some of you were even hypnotized or bitten by an abomination of a monster. We'll be talking to each class individually and takin' yer questions and concerns after this. Then we'll all have to decide how we deal with this unfortunate situation from here." He paused for a second, to make sure everyone was listening. "But right now, we have a special treat for ye, because ye've been through so very much. We're serving Five Flavored Soup, a recipe so delicious that it's better than anything ye've tasted at a restaurant—I guarantee it. This soup is a Finistere legend, and ye'll never taste its equal. Ms. Po, serve away!"

In no time, the Asian woman ladled soup as a dozen teachers handed them out to all of the students. If some students thought it was a little weird that we'd just been through the gauntlet and were now being served consolation-prize soup, nobody was showing it. Everyone was probably just too emotionally exhausted. When Mr. Lofting came over with the soup I got excited—a legendary recipe? I could probably deconstruct it in my mouth and copy it into my recipe book. But he yanked it back just as I was about to take it. "What was I thinking? No. You cannot eat this soup."

Once a few kids tried it and said it was the best soup they'd had in their life, everyone else got curious enough to give it a try, and soon all you could hear were loud slurps through the cafeteria. The teachers walked between the rows, looking up every so often and nodding at each other. Ms. Po looked up once she'd ladled the last of her soup, and Ms. Kahlo gave her a thumbs-up. I noticed that no teacher was touching the soup either. Brady and I just stared ahead, practically hypnotized by the noise. Slurp. Slurp. Slurp.

Gradually the slurping stopped, and one by one I watched every student rub their eyes or blink at the lights like they'd just woken up. "Where am I? What happened? Why are we in the cafeteria?" Every student asked some version of those questions. Brady gave me an impressed look and nodded. Then the nods became laughs. And then I couldn't help laughing too. We'd almost been bitten by a vampire, murdered by a werewolf, ripped apart by Frankenstein, captured by Invisible Man, and wrestled by a giant fish dude, but no one else was going to know.

As the kids all looked around confused, Ms. Po

walked over to us and smiled proudly. "An old family recipe," she said to me. I begged her to give it to me—imagine using this soup with Andy's guests—but she just giggled and shook her head. "I am the only one left who knows the recipe. Maybe one day, if you've had a really bad day, I will make it for you." Then she waddled off, carrying the big, empty soup pot.

"Students," Ms. Kahlo said, climbing onto an empty table. "It appears that our special guest speaker, Dr. Po, was too good of a hypnotist, and she hypnotized us all. What an incredible feat! Let's give a big hand to Dr. Po!" Ms. Po hobbled onto the table, now wearing a doctor's coat, and waved, thanking everyone as they gave her a confused round of applause. "Now let's all return to our classes," Ms. Calderon said. "And see if our memories return."

30

"So no one's going to remember any of that,"
Brady said, whistling as we made our way to the Council's
secret lounge. "That's just too perfect. You know, I don't
know how long this school could survive without teachers having a trick like that up their sleeve." She stopped
for a second, looked at me intensely, and said, "Hey, do
you think it's the first time they've pulled that? I mean,
the whole thing looked pretty rehearsed. That Ms. Po
looked like she's made that soup and worn that doctor's
coat before."

"Yeah." I nodded casually. "They must have pulled
that old amnesia soup trick plenty of times before. They
were all way too used to doing it." Then I realized what

she actually meant. "Oh, you mean, have we ever drank the soup before? Wow, good question. For all we know, we've been on death-defying adventures we don't even remember." I let that sink in. "That's spooky. File that under things to ask Gale when she's back."

"Javi and Brady, so delighted to have you with us." It was Mr. Bottom, smiling and bowing as he slid the bookshelf to the side and revealed the secret passage. "I hear that we owe our newfound freedom and peace to you. That was quite the winter of our discontent eh? My deepest and most heartfelt thanks. After you."

He motioned for us to head into the little passage-way, and after a short walk we were in the Council's chambers, with all five teachers gathered around their table, talking to Wiki. Wiki! I ran over and gave him another hug. It was as awkward as any human contact with Wiki gets, but I didn't care. The teachers then took turns thanking us or patting us on the backs, and then had us take seats at the table too.

"We thought it might be good to debrief," Ms. Kahlo said. "That was quite an adventure, quite a narrow escape, and something that we wish never to happen again."

"Seriously!" I said. "Could we spend a year without summoning legendary villains, maybe? Or maybe five years?" Ahab looked at me with steely eyes and I realized what Ms. Kahlo was actually saying. "Oh right, that was kinda sorta our fault. Heh heh. Sorry about that."

"Don't be so hard on yourself," Mr. Lofting said. "You made a tiny mistake leaving the bell out one night. And if you'd let her summon Dracula you were merely being empathetic and wanted Ms. Vlad to be happy. It was Dracula's fault, and his fault alone." Huh? That didn't make sense...

Ms. Love could tell that I was confused. "Thanks to Wiki's research and a conversation with Ms. Vlad, we have a sense of what happened. You see, many centuries ago Ms. Vlad was transformed into a vampire by Dracula, and the Count has a mental link to all of his victims. He can control their minds and also fool them into believing that he's a hero, not a monster. Ms. Vlad has always believed Dracula a hero whilst at Finistere, and has asked us to summon the vampire for many, many years. Gale has been smart enough to talk her out of it. But now we understand the reason. And now that Ms. Vlad has seen Dracula's true colors, she will not attempt to summon him again."

"So it's not our fault, but it's kind of our fault. But not really. Except it totally was." I was confusing myself!

"One thing is clear," Ms. Kahlo said. "The table is too great a temptation for you. It is not fair for you to have it at your house, for you shall always be tempted you to use it. It is frankly far too dangerous. We are going to move the table to Principal Gale's house when she returns."

"No!" Brady yelled. "You can't take Andy away! He's one of my best friends. He's like a cross between a pet, a table, and a BFF. I'll miss him too much!" She jumped out of her chair and her lip was quivering. Oh boy, here come the waterworks.

We spent the next few minutes figuring out the arrangement. The three of us could visit Andy whenever we wanted and hang out with him as long as we wanted, but it would have to be at Ms. Gale's house. Ms. Kahlo explained that it'd be like having a best friend who lived at your house for a while, but was now moving back to his own house. Since we had unlimited visiting privileges, I wasn't too worried about the situation. I was sure Gale would let me host dinner parties whenever I wanted. Plus, I've always been super curious about what Ms. Gale's house looks like. Do her flying monkeys just flit around her living room? Does the Cowardly Lion secretly live in the basement?

"Now that it's settled, onto the fun part," Mr. Bottom said, smiling broadly. "Please recount your adventure to us in full. How did you make it through the snowstorm, infiltrate the castle, and defeat the monsters?" Mr. Bottom took a quill from the table and put a piece of paper in front of him. Was he going to take notes? Was Mr. B a writer? I asked him and he smiled, winked, and said, "I dabble."

Wiki, Brady, and I took turns telling the story. We were all so energized by our victory that we got really into it, basically acting out the entire thing in front of them. My favorite part was watching Wiki attempt to do an impression of Fish Dude. Brady's impression of Toastito was pretty spot-on too. When we got to the Invisible Man and Werewolf battles, we were all jumping around pretending to be monsters and choreographing our epic battles. Then the boss fight came and Brady interrupted my baguette sword fight.

"Hey, we never talked about how you beat Dracula. Anyone else find it super weird that Javi took out the most epic monster of all time with a baguette? I mean, yeah, plenty of strange things went down today— invisible guys, fish-human hybrids, a nerd from a computer manual attacking a mannequin—but defeating a vampire with bread kind of takes the cake." I smirked the smuggest smirk and opened my mouth to answer her.

"We had the same question, lad," Ahab said, reaching under the table and pulling out a chunk of baguette, "and when we asked Vlad, she had us taste it and figure it out for ourselves. Try it yourself." Brady took the chunk slowly, looking at me like I poisoned it.

"Garlic," I said as she bit down and nodded. "Not bad for a C+ human, eh? You know, if this story ever gets out, can we please pretend that I used a real sword and not a baguette? It feels a lot less epic defeating the final boss with a loaf of bread." We all had a good laugh.

"Your cooking saved the day," Mr. Bottom said. "Many

a chef can win a cooking contest, but I know no chefs who've defeated a gang of monsters with their delectable cuisine." I blushed.

"It's best you get back to class now, so nobody's suspicious," Ms. Calderon said. "Remember, not a word of this to anyone. And be kind to Ms. Vlad. She's being very hard on herself after the whole incident. She does not realize that she isn't to blame."

We nodded and walked back to class, feeling a teensy bit bummed that no one had any idea that we'd saved all of their butts.

31

A week later there was a knock on my door.
The guest of honor had arrived. "Wiki! Welcome to your
"Sorry I Was Wrong, Thank You For Putting Up With My
Dumb Ideas" dinner. And a big welcome to you too, Aunt
Nancy." Wiki walked through the door semi-suspicious,
but Aunt Nancy nudged him into our house and gave
me a big smile.

"I know that smell," Wiki said, brightening up
immediately. "But it's so overpowering." He made his
way to the dining room. "Javi, how much mofongo did
you make?" Then he rounded the corner to see Mount
Mofongo. I can't even begin to count the time it took me
or the money I spent on plantains (the teachers helped)

but taking up a huge chunk of Andy was my delicious, ridiculous centerpiece: a three-foot-tall mountain of delectable, garlicky mofongo. Mashed, fried plantains never looked so epic. "Javi..." he said, standing over the mountain and taking a long, long whiff. "This is heaven."

"You deserve it," I said. "You warned us like you always do, we ignored you like we always do, but this time it almost resulted in a full-on vampire apocalypse. Now let's eat! It'll only be a few more days until we have to give Andy to Principal Gale, so I want to get one last epic dinner in."

Mount Mofongo was also my official Return of Chef Javi comeback party. Is it weirder that it took a naked, invisible guy praising my food to make me realize I hadn't lost my touch, or that almost killing a vampire with my garlic bread also helped? Either way, I was done feeling sorry for myself. Save the world once and that's luck. Save it twice and, hey, maybe you're not the ultimate failure or a C+ human.

"Is it finally time? My mouth's been watering for hours!" Brady practically flew down the stairs. She ran over to Wiki, gave him the awkwardest I'm Sorry hug, and sat down, trying to figure out how she was going to get a chunk of that mountain on her plate. "Hey, what's with the extra seats?" Aunt Nancy and I looked at each other and giggled.

"Well, there's no way four of us can tackle this mountain of mofongo alone. I invited a few special guests. One more should be getting here the normal way..." As if on cue, the doorbell rang, and I let Mr. Lofting in. Brady and Wiki were super happy to see him—everyone loves Mr. Lofting. They chatted for a bit, before Wiki asked me the inevitable question—who were the other guests? And that's when I dramatically pulled the bell out from behind my back and summoned our pals.

And by pals, I mean monsters. The light flashed, the pop was extra loud, and sitting next to us were none other than Fish Dude, Werewolf Guy, and Frankenstein. Wiki and Brady jumped out of their chairs, Wiki using his like a lion tamer at a circus. "Have you gone completely insane?" Wiki screamed. "Invite the good guys! Not the villains!"

"Villains?" Werewolf Guy said. "Whoa whoa whoa. I'm a mild-mannered sub who volunteers at my local soup kitchen on the weekends. There's nothing villainous about me. Apparently I've got a really weird sickness, but my wife has figured out a way to keep me from doing any damage on full moons." He looked over at me proudly. "Silver handcuffs. Apparently all I do now is howl."

"And I hope, friend William, that you weren't for even a moment referring to me as a villain," Frankenstein said politely as he served himself some mofongo. "My unfortunate past is behind me, and I shall be starting over with a clean slate. I took your advice and read the rest of my story. It appears I was about to do some unspeakable things. But here I shall live peacefully and strive to better my community."

"Grrawrgh! Rarrgh!" Fish Dude did his loud burp-talk and reminded Wiki and Brady who they were actually afraid of. They both eyed him suspiciously, waiting for him to attack.

"He says, 'I apologize for my loudness and my tone of voice. If I seem frustrated all the time, it's because I've had an itch on my back as long as I can remember, and I can't ever quite seem to reach it. But no one understands what I'm saying, so they can't help either,'" Mr. Lofting said. Brady, Wiki, and Fish Dude's jaw's dropping at the exact same time.

Aunt Nancy laughed hysterically. "Oh, it was worth it, Dolittle! I'm so glad you were game to attend our little dinner." She chuckled a bit more and then pointed her fork at Mr. Lofting. "Our dear Mr. Lofting is none other than Dr. Dolittle, who speaks to animals. Didn't you find his class pets a little too smart? It's because they're in constant conversation. In any event, I thought our scaly friend here could use a little translation."

After everyone recovered from the shock, Brady went over, figured out where he itched, and scratched it for a while. Fish Dude gave the most satisfied sigh you can imagine from an enormous fish-person. "Grrrrawrgh! Grrrrrrrrawrgh!" he burped. "He thanks you profusely," said Mr. Lofting. "If ever you need swimming lessons, or you lose something in a pool or lake, he's your guy, he says."

I stood up and tapped on my glass. "Let the Mofongo

Mountain Monster Mayhem begin!" I started serving everyone generous chunks of mofongo and, as expected, it was everyone's favorite food ever. (Except maybe Fish Dude, who's probably got a very different palate than the rest of us.) "I apologize that we couldn't invite our dear friend Dracula, but there are probably twenty garlic cloves in this, so it would've been torture."

"You wouldn't have..." Wiki said, horrified, and the rest of us laughed.

We ate until we practically fell over, and between Mr. Lofting's hilarious stories about his adventures with Dab-Dab and the gang, and Fish Dude's horrible celebrity impressions, it might have been the most entertaining dinner party I've ever had.

"If I may," Aunt Nancy said, clinking her glass until all eyes were on her. "I'd like to have a moment of silence."

"For who?" Brady asked. "I'm pretty sure we all made it out alive."

"Not for who. For what," Aunt Nancy said, winking as she put her finger to her lips. We all shut up and stared at each other until Aunt Nancy tapped her ear. What was she hearing that we weren't? It took me a full minute and it was very faint, but I jumped out of my seat when I heard it.

"Did you put on Dad's coqui sounds album?" Brady asked. She heard it too.

"As the two of you know," Aunt Nancy said, "there are very few places in the world where coqui can survive, and most of them live in Puerto Rico. I thought Dracula's tiny amphibian friends might have a place in our forest." I ran over and gave her a huge hug. I didn't care if I looked ridiculous, hearing those little frogs immediately doubled my quality of life. Plus, I couldn't wait to see Dad's reaction when he heard it. Brady kept everyone from talking for a full five minutes so we could hear their symphony of croaks.

After who knows how long, Aunt Nancy gave me a nod, and I pulled the bell out again.

"And now, for the moment we've all been waiting for. Andy, bring back Principal Gale!"

Poof! Pop! Sitting in the last empty chair was our dear, dear principal. Except she was dressed in a poufy, glittery emerald gown with a green tiara in her hair and green glasses.

"Oh! Hello everyone. My oh my, I was just at a banquet for our dear friend Betsy Bobbin. It's quite shocking to go from eating with talking animals to a room full of normal...people?" As she slowly looked around the room, she realized that this was probably a weirder bunch than the Oz folks, and we all laughed hysterically. Her face was priceless.

"Oh Gale, we have quite a lot to catch you up on," Aunt Nancy said in between giggles. "But for now, feel free to attack Mount Mofongo and eat up. You won't find better food in this world or Oz, I can tell you that."

"One thing that's been puzzling me since you left," Wiki said, pointing a fork toward the principal. "Why Ms. Vlad? Of every teacher at Finistere, why did you pick her?"

"Dolengen is an honorable, trustworthy friend with a strong moral compass," Principal Gale said slowly. "But, if you must know, she was the only one brave enough to volunteer for the task." She gave Wiki a big smile before diving into the mofongo.

"So," I said, between too-big bites, "I guess the lesson here is that everyone is exactly as they appear. Dracula was bad just like expected, even though Ms. Vlad said otherwise. People's reputations are always accurate, and we should judge them before we meet them."

"What? No, Javi," Brady said, shaking her head and rolling her eyes in her signature style. "That's because Dracula was using mind control. He doesn't count. Look at everyone else. Frankenstein is the nicest guy, even though they say he's a monster, Fish Man is just itchy and misunderstood, Werewolf is a super sweetie... I mean, we're eating dinner with a trio that terrifies most people."

"Brady," I said, munching through a big pile of mofongo before I continued. "That was a joke. Now, who wants to learn a brand-new dance? Anyone heard of the Monster Mash?"

I blasted the song through the speakers and it truly was a graveyard smash.

WIKI'S PEDIA

Extra intel on our visitors from Wiki's notebooks.

COUNT DRACULA

The count who kick-started the world's obsession with bloodsuckers, Dracula is a centuries-old Transylvanian vampire with plans of world domination. In the 1897 novel *Dracula*, the Count heads to England to attempt to turn everyone into vampires, but is thwarted by a team led by Dr. Van Helsing. The original Count Dracula is stronger than twenty men, can assume the form of a wolf or bat, and can control the weather. Some aspects of the character were likely inspired by fifteenth-century Vlad the Impaler, who was also known as Dracula.

ADA LOVELACE (MS. LOVE)

A math whiz and science genius, Ada Lovelace is considered by many to be the world's first computer programmer. She was born August Ada King, Countess of Lovelace, the daughter of the famous poet Lord Byron. Ada is most well-known for her work on mathematician Charles Babbage's mechanical computer, the Analytical Engine. She wrote a series of commands for Babbage's computer, which turned out to be the first computer program ever written. Ada also correctly predicted that computers would one day compose music, create graphics, and benefit science greatly. Fun fact—Ada's father: Lord Byron inspired Mary Shelley to write the book *Frankenstein*.

DR. DOLITTLE (DR. LOFTING)

Dr. Dolittle is the main character in a series of children's books by Hugh Lofting. Though Dolittle started his career as a physician, his parrot, Polynesia, taught him how to speak to animals, and he became a brilliant veterinarian respected by creatures from around the world. Dolittle lives in Puddleby-on-the-Marsh, where his housekeeper Dab-Dab is a duck and his visitors and patients are animals.

THE CHESHIRE CAT

The Cheshire Cat is a fictional feline who appears in Lewis Carroll's *Alice's Adventures in Wonderland*. He's best known for his broad, mischievous grin and his ability to disappear and reappear at will, sometimes leaving his grin behind. The Cheshire Cat helps Alice figure out how things work in Wonderland, but speaks in riddles, often baffling Alice.

CONAN THE BARBARIAN

Conan is a fictional barbarian whose fantasy adventures take place in the prehistoric past. Created by Robert E. Howard in 1932, Conan wanders the world in search of adventure, encountering monsters, evil sorcerers, epic heroes, and nefarious villains along the way. The brawny warrior originated in a series of short stories, but his tales have since been adapted to books, comics, movies, TV, and video games.

MENG PO

Meng Po is the goddess of forgetfulness in Chinese mythology. She collects herbs from all over the world to create a special soup that erases the memory of anyone who drinks it. This allows a person to reincarnate into the next life without the worries of their previous life. Meng Po serves her special soup on the Bridge of Forgetfulness. In Chinese tradition, there are legends of miracle babies born speaking because the baby's soul didn't drink the soup.

SACAGAWEA

Sacagawea was a Shoshone woman who helped the explorers Lewis and Clark travel thousands of miles—from North Dakota to the Pacific Ocean—on their historic expedition to explore and map the western half of America. She served as a translator, guide, and peacekeeper when they encountered other Native Americans. Sacagawea made the expedition at age sixteen, while caring for her newborn son.

ACKNOWLEDGMENTS

This villainous escapade wouldn't exist if not for these folks, the least monstrous people that I know. Thank you for being so emphatically non-monstrous.

First and foremost, my phenomenal agent, Elana Roth Parker, and my incredible editor, Annie Berger, for helping me build a solid enough foundation with book one that the sequel was a pure joy to write.

Evelyn, for the endless support and for offering to read every single draft.

Juan Carlos, for the inspiration, motivation, and pep talks.

Mami and Papi, for instilling the rabid curiosity that makes researching these books a blast.

Jamie and Keren, who read them all and point a way forward.

Chris and Greg, for the walks and the jokes.

Ivan and Jeremy, for the past and future collabs.

Andrew and Andy, for the adventures and encouragement.

All the friends and family who came out of the woodwork to support the first book—you completely made my year. What an unexpected, magical surprise. Valeria Rodriguez Sisson, Alejandra Rodriguez Mullett, Randee Dawn, Fran & Jim O'Hara, Taylor Piñeiro, Alicia and Jimmy O'Hara, Jeannie Gallego, Joe Prota, Julianne Faris Kur, Brittany Garrett, Jason Ferguson, Janine Ramos, Jax Villalobos, Rachelle Digregorio, Jason Griffin, Michael McWatters, Adam Hann-Byrd, Alyssa Palermo, Nathan Peters, Titi Yvonne, Titi Barbara, Tio Eric, Marlena Ryan, Trish Milano, Antonio Garza, Kacy Emmett, Austin Powe, Marnie Thompson, Brandt Hamilton, and Brian Weinstein.

The author friends I made this year, thank you for the unbelievable support! I'm looking at you, Joshua S. Levy, Sam Subity, Megan E. Freeman, Halli Gomez, Alyssa Wishingrad, Ben Gartner, Nate Cernosek, Shawn Peters, Krista Van Dolzer, Joanne Rossmassler

Fritz, Cliff Burke, Shakirah Bourne, and the whole 21ders crew.

Ashlyn Keil, Caitlin Lawler, Margaret Coffee, Michelle Mayhall, Chelsey Moler Ford, Susan Barnett, Lizzie Lewandowski, David Miles, Nicole Hower, and the rest of the incredible Sourcebooks team, who continue to dazzle me with their brilliance.

And especially Florence, Miles, Liam, Nora, Julian, and Luke, the greatest kids I know.

"Ahem," you say. "You forgot about the part where you tell us who you're inviting to dinner."

You know what? This time, I'm curious who you would invite to dinner. I've got this mountain of mofongo in my kitchen that needs to be devoured.

ABOUT THE AUTHOR

Victor Piñeiro is a creative director and content strategist who's worked at HBO Max, managed @YouTube and launched @Skittles, creating its award-winning zany voice. He's also designed games for Hasbro, written/produced a documentary on virtual worlds, and taught third graders. *Monster Problems* is his second novel.

Before Javi and his friends had monster problems, they had to deal with...**TIME VILLAINS!**

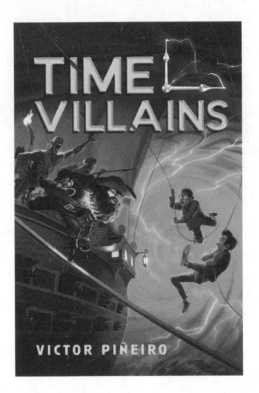

"You won't be able to put down this action-packed, relentlessly funny adventure."

— Sarah Mlynowski, author of the *New York Times* bestselling Whatever After series